BOUND FOR TEXAS

_____

KIT PRATE

WOLFPACK
PUBLISHING
— EST 2013 —

WOLFPACK
PUBLISHING
— EST 2013 —

Bound For Texas

Wolfpack Publishing
6032 Wheat Penny Avenue
Las Vegas, NV 89122

wolfpackpublishing.com

Paperback ISBN 978-1-64734-147-3
eBook ISBN 978-1-64734-146-6

BOUND FOR TEXAS

CHAPTER 1

Liberty lay wasting beneath the blue-white heat of a noon sun, sprawled out like a man dying from heat stroke. The railroad track spine shimmered, pulsing mirror-bright flashes reminiscent of a signalman's heliograph. Absently, Belden pushed aside the lace curtain and tried to make sense out of the dot-dash pattern. *After all these years,* he mused. *The War was almost eight years behind him, and yet...* He tore his gaze away from the steel rails and forced the old memories back into the dark closets of his mind, concentrating on the people moving up and down the main street.

There were children in the street; Saturday children. Bare-headed and bare-footed, they hop-scotched down the dirt street, moving like water popping in hot grease. Belden grinned, watching as they ran from one shade spot to another, pausing to crinkle their toes in the cool earth before moving on. He watched as a young boy raced across the sunbaked *caliche* and paused to dangle his feet in a watering trough, the youngster finally easing over the wooden edge to submerge himself neck deep in the brackish water. The boy's escape from the sun was brief, his horrified mother yanking him bodily from the tank and marching him down the hot board walk. Reluctantly, feeling a man's sympathy for a boy's misery, Belden pushed the curtain back in place.

He was big, broad shouldered and long limbed, with the deep tan of a man accustomed to long hours under the sun; uncomfortable and out of place among the potted ferns and marble statuary that surrounded him. Impatient, he lifted his hand, smoothing his hair. The fingers arched, and he scratched the spot behind his left ear where the cord from the eye patch had eroded its thin groove.

"It's pure Hell, ain't it? All this waiting?" Lon Belden lounged against the far wall; at fifteen, a younger, and more compact version of the other. Seventeen years separated the brothers; that, and a difference in temperament and experience that creased one's face with the hardness of times gone by, and this one with the quick lines of boyish laughter.

"Quit saying ain't and stop swearing." Trace spoke with a tired impatience, his voice taking on the tone of a weary parent.

"You could have left me with the crew." Lon's head came forward slightly as he tugged at his tight collar. An oily smear spotted the mirror that hung on the wall at his back. He saw the spot and tried to rub it away with his sleeve, succeeding only in making it bigger.

"Sure," Trace said ruefully. "I left you with them. Last night. That's why I had to bail you out of jail this morning."

Lon grinned across at his brother. "We had one grand old time, Trace," he said, his face coloring. "There's this girl down at that *cantina* by the tracks got…" He cupped his hands in front of him.

"Madam will see you now." A strange voice cut into the young man's remembrances; clipped, precise. Disapproving. "If you… *gentleman* will follow me." The man gestured for them to fall in behind him, his nose in the air as if he smelled something unpleasant. Lon shoved himself away from the wall and shouldered his way past Trace, imitating the butler's mincing walk. Belden lifted a well-polished boot and applied it to the kid's rear end.

The woman was waiting for them in the parlor, standing in front of the marble mantled fireplace. Poised; attractive in the way a woman of means is attractive, she was wearing a pale green dress, brocaded with touches of deep green velvet on the bodice and sleeves. The green accented her hazel eyes, set off her deep auburn hair. She reached out a pale hand. "Trace," the greeting was cordial but strained, her eyes staring somewhere past the man. A smile formed as she recognized the youth that was standing behind the man, and it was almost sincere. "Lonny!?" She measured the boy with an approving eye. "You've changed, Lon."

"You haven't," Lon answered, ignoring the baleful look his brother flashed at him. There was nothing complimentary in the boy's tone; none intended. He helped himself to an apple from the bowl on the table, wiping the fruit on his shirt front, and flopped into a chair.

The woman's brow knotted, and she inhaled sharply, unsure of the boy's meaning. Lips tight, she dismissed him from her thoughts and faced Belden. "You look well, Trace." She allowed her eyes to drift over his face and felt the familiar tightness in her chest, a warm flush coloring her cheeks. The animal sensuality that had always marked the man was still there, unchanged by the passage of time or the ravages of war. If anything, the dark good looks that had attracted her as a young girl had increased; the subtle molding of his features enhanced by the eye patch that covered his right eye. The black patch gave him the look of a rogue, a jaded hero from the pages of the fictional romance serials she so enjoyed. Even his hair, flecked with a salting of silver, and the carefully trimmed mustache, added to the rugged handsomeness. She composed herself and reached for the velveteen cord that hung on the wall at her right. "I thought perhaps we could have some sherry…"

"No, thank you." Belden's voice was soft. Too soft. He had no patience for the pretentious formality he found in this place or for the polite niceties the woman was attempting to force on him. There was more. The huskiness in her voice that stoked a fire Belden had thought long dead; a fire that tied knots deep in his belly and bristled the hair at the back of his neck. He fought the memory of what lay buried beneath the thick folds of her gown. "I want to see Adam, Elizabeth," he said. "Now."

The woman stiffened, recognizing the man's tone. "It's been a long time, Trace." She lifted her green cat eyes to look at him fully, her petite features becoming hawk like. "You can't expect to come here and just…"

"I expect to see my son," the man interrupted softly, "just like the attorneys arranged." He took a step toward the woman. "No excuses this time, Elizabeth. No stories about how you didn't know I was coming, no last-minute emergency trips out of town…" Belden was displaying a vast amount of control he did not feel, remembering all the times in the past the planned meetings had failed to transpire. "I want to see my son," he repeated. He was beside the woman now, towering above her, the sweet scent of her cologne tempting him.

"Trace." The voice came from the hallway. Cord Bishop came through the doorway, his hand extended in greeting, a wan smile pasted across his lips.

Belden faced the man; purposely ignoring Bishop's outstretched hand. There was an awkward silence, interrupted by the whispered cursing of Belden's younger brother. Lon rose up out of his chair. Trace waved him back into his seat, shaking his head. "Cord," he greeted. There was no animosity in his voice; no bitterness; nothing to reveal the instant surge of anger that flowed through him.

Bishop moved across the room, stopping to give his wife a dutiful peck on her rouged cheek before going to the decanter of brandy on the mahogany table. "We received your letter, Trace," he poured himself a drink, lifting the glass in a silent invitation, "and, of course, the letter from your attorney…" The liquor seemed to lose its appeal when Belden shook his head in refusal, and he set his untouched glass back on the silver tray. "About the boy," he began, apprehensive.

"About *my* son," Belden corrected.

Bishop sighed, a long quavering sound, his hand going to his forehead. "Leave us, Elizabeth. Please." The man seemed to age visibly, his shoulders sagging. She started toward him; her arms outstretched, and then reconsidered and withdrew, pulling the pocket doors together as she departed. He stared after her, silent, his eyes still on the closed panels as he began to speak. "I'm not a man ac- customed to begging, Trace. You above all men should know that…" He swung his head toward Belden. "Leave the boy be, Trace," he implored. His face crumpled, and it took a great effort for the man to regain his composure. He changed his mind about the brandy and picked up the glass, his hand shaking. "He's all we have, Trace. All we have," he finished weakly.

"Elizabeth was with child when the two of you left Laredo, Cord." Belden's words came through clenched teeth, the memory kindling the anger that was welling within him. "*Your child.*"

"We lost him, Trace." Bishop said the words as though he expected, and deserved, sympathy from the man. He poured himself a second drink, and then another, and wiped his mouth with the back of his hand. "He was born dead," he whispered. "Not even a first cry…" He faced Belden, the agony deep in his eyes. "There can never be another," he choked. "Never!"

Belden inhaled, secretly enjoying the other man's torment. The passing years had left their mark on Bishop. He was soft; his outer shell slack and portly and the inner core bearing no resemblance to the man Belden remembered. The rage that had been clawing at Belden's insides began the slow climb up his throat. "If I remember my Old Testament, Cord, God dealt with David in much the same way." He laughed, no humor in the sound. "You do remember David, Cord?" he asked, his tone caustic. "He slept with the wife of one of his soldiers and decided he wanted her for his own." He fingered the black patch that covered his blind eye. "Then he sent that man into battle," he continued, his voice a strained monotone, "arranged for him to die.

"Like you sent me, Cord." Belden's voice shook, and he reached out, grabbing the man's coat. "Only I came back!" He slammed Bishop against the fireplace, twisting the man's jacket tight around his neck. "You took my wife, Cord! *I'm not going to let you have my son!!*" There was a scream from the doorway at Belden's back, the high-pitched noise of a woman's shrill voice.

Elizabeth stood in the doorway, framed by the light from the hall windows, her right hand at her throat, her left tightly clenched on the shoulder of the young boy that stood in front of her. For a long agonizing moment, the three faced each other.

The child moved. He darted across the room, crying, his fists waving wildly in the air. Belden reached out to him and felt the boy's fists beating a weak tattoo against his chest and shoulders. "Adam," he pleaded softly. He lifted the boy off his feet and stared into his flushed face and saw not one mote of recognition. "Adam," he repeated the word.

"You hurt my Pa!" The child's pale hands slapped at Belden's face. "*You hurt my Pa*!!"

Stunned, Belden placed the boy on the floor and stepped back. Elizabeth was at the boy's side, Cord Bishop behind them. The woman smiled at him, a look of smug self-satis-faction filling her green eyes. "I think it would be best if you leave, Mr. Belden." There was an arrogance in her, a haugh-tiness that came with the conceit of winning. She caressed her son's shoulder, a proprietary manner in her touch. The cold smile grew. "Say goodbye to Mr. Belden, Adam."

The boy's eyes narrowed and his lower lip jutted out in a gesture of belligerent dislike. His voice was sullen. "Goodbye, Mr. Belden."

Trace stared down at the boy, a pain deep in his chest that was threatening to suffocate him. *Goodbye, Mr. Belden.* The boy's words stung him with the same fire as a hot branding iron. There was no warmth in the boy's eyes, no indication that he had any desire to remember anything or anyone beyond the confines of this house. There was only hatred; the same hatred Belden had seen in the woman's eyes. *As if he and the boy were total strangers and there was no kinship, no father and son bond of blood.* "Goodbye, Adam," Belden breathed, extending his hand. The boy backed away from him, his small hand lifting instead to grasp at Cord Bishop's fingers.

"Trace," Lon was on his feet, his face white.

Belden shook his head at the youth. "We're leaving, Lon. Now." He headed for the front door.

Lon studied the trio that stood in front of the fireplace, examining their faces. Bishop first, the pompous piece of shit that seemed to be hiding behind the woman; and then the boy, who looked – he realized – nothing at all like Trace. His gaze finally rested on the woman. "You bitch," he whispered. "*You filthy bitch*!"

******

Lincoln McLane strode the length of the narrow barroom, Charlie Fletcher at his side, the lawman adjusting his long gait to compensate for the other man's stiff-legged limp. He headed directly for the table in the far corner at the back of the room; the only table – after a long, busy night – that was still occupied. "Trace," he nodded, touching the brim of his hat in greeting.

Belden stared up at the man, his vision fogged by the whiskey. He'd been in the saloon the entire night. The rooms upstairs first, and then later, the bar. He shrugged and shoved out a chair. "I'm buying, Linc."

McLane ignored the man's invitation. "So I heard." He jerked his head at his companion. "Charlie says you've been buyin' pretty steady for the past two days."

Trace sighed, both hands locked around his glass. "Charlie was one fine sergeant, Linc." He lifted his good eye to his foreman. "Always wet-nursing the men." His voice took on an edge. "Sometimes, even the officers."

Fletcher ignored Belden's sarcasm. "Only when they needed it," he growled. He pulled out the chair directly opposite Belden and sat down. "Tell him, Linc," he ordered.

McLane dug into his shirt pocket. "I've got a complaint here, filed by Cord Bishop and his wife. They claim you created a disturbance in their home, made some threats…"

Belden poured himself one more drink and slid the bottle across the table. "That was two days ago," he interrupted. "You try and push that paper, and I'm just liable to push back."

McLane sucked in a lung full of air, his face turning a mottled purple. "Damn it, Trace," he breathed. "I didn't say anything about pushing." He toed out a chair and sat down. "I heard about your boy, about what happened." He raised his hand when Belden attempted to speak. "This is Bishop's town, Trace," he warned, keeping the words private. "What Cord doesn't own outright, he holds the paper on…"

"Like he owns you?" Belden smiled the accusation, but there was no mirth in the words.

The lawman tensed, fingering the badge that hung from his lapel. He reached out, grabbing Belden's arm when the other man started to pour yet another drink. "You've got cattle due in, Trace. Today. I want them unloaded, and you and your outfit out of here. Tomorrow."

Trace wrenched his arm free and downed the whiskey. "Go to Hell, Linc."

McLane was angry, and the anger was in his voice, his sudden stiff-backed posture. "Lon is making noises, Trace. He's been shooting his mouth off all over town. He braced Bishop outside the bank this morning, told him that if he and the woman don't give up the boy, he's going to ride in there and take him." The lawman grinned into Belden's face, the smile not quite reaching his eyes.

Trace considered the lawman's words, his brow furrowing. "I can handle Lon." He made a circle with his finger on the rim of his glass. "I can handle Lon," he repeated, this time with more conviction.

Charlie Fletcher snorted, daring to trespass in a way no other man would risk. "Sure you can!" he said contemptuously. "You can't even handle yourself! You've been drunk the last two days, and the kid ain't much better."

He reached out, his hand on Belden's sleeve. "You can't change any of it, Trace. Not Elizabeth; not the boy. Give it up," he advised.

Belden's jaws tightened. He was remembering the confrontation with the woman, with Bishop, with his son. There was a gnawing pain deep in his chest, the same ache he had tried to kill with the whiskey. "Let's go find Lon, Charlie," he said. He got to his feet slowly, and the pain rose with him. He wondered if it would ever leave him.

******

Lon Belden lay stretched out on the bed, his arms behind his head, his eyes screwed shut against the glare of the risen sun. He was aware of the murmur of voices in the other room; the soft mumble that was Fletcher's and the deeper, clear sound of his brother. *Trace.* They had been together, sometime during the previous night. Or the night before. The boy couldn't be sure, his thoughts and memories clouded by the same whiskey that was tearing at his intestines.

A chair scraped across the floor of the adjoining room, and there was the sound of heavy footsteps coming across the wooden floor. The youth fluffed his pillow and turned his face to the wall, feigning sleep.

Trace came into the room and stood at the foot of the bed, looking down at the boy. He spied the pitcher of water on the washstand, smiling at the idea that played across his mind. Picking up the container, he dumped its contents down the back of the sleeping youngster and stepped back. The results were fascinating.

"*Goddamnmiserableson-of-a-bitch*!!" The curses came as one long word as Lon bolted out of the bed, swinging wildly. Trace held him at arm's length, letting go just as Lon lunged forward with a mighty swing. The boy sprawled flat on his face on the rough wooden floor.

"I thought you got all of that out of your system when I hauled you out of that bar." Belden shook his head, watching as his brother pulled himself up on his knees.

Lou crawled up onto the bed, his face white, and both hands clutching his belly. "I don't feel so good."

Trace looked down at the boy, feeling no sympathy at his condition, his own stomach still tender. He reached out a long leg and kicked the door shut. "We've got cows due in, Lon. You're going to help me unload 'em." Belden unwrapped a foul-looking cigar and moistened it end to end with his tongue. He lit up, gazing at the boy through a thin haze of blue smoke. "Get dressed," he ordered.

"I told you. I don't feel good!" The boy looked up at his brother, angry.

"You've got a bad case of the horrors." Belden exhaled with slow purpose. "Too much rotgut in an empty belly." He nodded toward the closed window. "A day in the air, a little sunshine, will sweat it right out of you. You'll be feeling good as new in no time," he lied.

Lon shook his head, cradling the pillow against his sore stomach. The air in the room felt used, the dense smoke from his brother's cigar beginning to hang in heavy blue layers. "I'm sick," he croaked. His face was an ash grey, dark circles under his eyes. He threw the pillow on the floor and jumped up from the bed, charging toward the window. The warped frame howled in protest as he forced the window open, jamming midway as the sash refused to yield. Desperate, the youth wedged his head sideways through the narrow opening. He was sick; violently, his stomach contracting against his backbone as he vomited, the room filling with the stench of bile and regurgitated whiskey.

Belden kept puffing on the cigar, quiet. He went over to the bed and picked up the boy's pillow, pulling off the water-soaked casing. When the kid pulled his head in the window, Belden grabbed him. "We're going to talk, Lonny." He wiped the damp cloth across the boy's face and neck, his fist knotted in a thick tangle of dark hair. "About your drinking and about your mouth." He gave the kid's face one more rough swipe before letting go of the clump of hair.

"*Maldito*, Trace! That hurt!!" The boy was standing in the middle of the room, rubbing the top of his head. His color was improving, his cheeks taking on the red flush of wind burn. He dropped his hand to his stomach, the slow grin creasing the skin behind his ears. "Sure hope there wasn't anybody on the walk when I got sick." The kid was healing fast, his fingers massaging his now empty belly. "What's for breakfast?"

Belden sighed. Only the very young recovered so rapidly. It seemed such a waste. "The crew had breakfast hours ago," he tossed the boy his pants, his tone vindictive.

Lon pulled on the jeans, his toenails scraping against the stiff denim. "I want a steak, and a dozen eggs." He fastened his belt and then unpeeled his soiled shirt, his head disappearing. "And a gallon of milk," he said, the words muffled as he poked his head into a fresh work shirt. "You buyin'?"

"Lunch," Belden answered. He chewed on his cigar and leaned back, his elbows resting on the dresser. The boy started to argue, and Belden raised his hand. "I saw McLane. He said that you've been raising hell all over town."

"So?" Lon was on the bed, tugging at his boots. He stood up, stamping his foot as he forced his heel into the stiff leather.

Belden chewed a bit harder on the cigar. "So he told me about you and Cord Bishop," he said matter-of-factly.

Lon was at the window, his eyes on the street; one finger tracing his initials on the dirt-caked glass. "You tell that bastard it isn't any of his business?" he asked.

"I told him I'd take care of it," Trace answered. He took the cigar out of his mouth and studied the burning tip. "I told him that I'd take care of *you*," he said finally.

Lon was careful to keep his eyes on the activity in the crowded street below. "I don't need any goddamn keeper," he breathed.

Belden was still eyeing the smoldering stub of his cigar. He smashed the foul-smelling cheroot in the basin at his elbow and picked up the bar of soap from the dish. "Lonny!" He tossed the cake of lye to his brother.

Startled, Lon turned. Instinctively, he flung out both hands, his fingers closing around the slippery mass. "What the Hell…?"

Trace pushed himself away from the dresser. "I was just about your age when Pa took me down and scrubbed my mouth out with a chunk of soap twice that size." He pointed a finger at the boy. "For saying shit when a draft horse with a foot the size of a bucket stomped on my big toe." He shook his head at the memory, his stomach rolling. "I was sick for a week." He continued. "I'm getting tired of your big mouth, Lonny; tired of hauling your butt out of saloons because you haven't got sense to say sober." He was quiet, his gaze riveted on the boy's face. "It's going to stop, Lon. The loud mouth, the drinking. The helling around."

The boy averted his eyes, unable to meet the steady scrutiny of his brother's stare. "And the rest of the crew. You gonna stop them too?" There was open hostility in the boy's words. He heaved the cake of soap at the far wall. The bar thudded against the peeling paper, suspended for a time before sliding to the floor.

"The rest of the crew is full grown, Lonny." Belden's rebuke carried a sting, and he saw the boy's fists knot. "They do a man's job, and draw a man's pay. That buys them the rights to a man's pleasures."

"I draw wages, Trace." Lon's face was white, his jaws set.

It was an old argument, one Belden had heard too many times in the past six weeks. "Wrangler's wages, Lon," he said, tired; sorry now that he had allowed the youth to come along on the drive. "The same wages I'd pay any green kid." There was a long silence between the two, the youth smarting from the man's reprimand. He started to speak, the words dying on his lips when Belden raked him with a long, cold stare. "I'm not going to argue with you, boy," Belden crossed the room to the window, towering above the kid. "No more trouble, Lonny."

Still defiant, the boy stared up into his brother's face. "Bullshit!" His face coloring, he dropped his head, the frown turning into a little-boy pout. He swore again, under his breath, and headed for the door.

Belden reached out, hauling him back. "I meant what I said, Lon. Every word." Satisfied the boy finally understood, he let go.

CHAPTER 2

———

They were on the platform waiting for the train, Belden pacing the length of the plank landing with a long military stride. Lon pulled his makings from his pocket and began building a smoke, the thin tissue fluttering in the wind. Belden heard the soft whisper of the paper and turned, a frown pulling at the corners of his mouth. "Give it here, Lon."

"It was for you," the youth said, avoiding his brother's gaze.

"Sure," Belden answered. He held out his hand, taking the cigarette, keeping the hand extended until the boy surrendered the tobacco and papers as well. Satisfied, he scraped his thumb nail across the blue tip of a wooden match, and the stick came alive; the smell of sulfur on the warm air. He inhaled and coughed, holding the cigarette an arm's length away as he studied it. "What is this?" he demanded, the air filled with the pungent aroma of *marijuana*.

Lon dropped his head, hiding a grin. He shrugged. "Just something I picked up over in Grease Town," he said innocently.

Belden crushed the smoke out between his gloved fingers and tossed the unsmoked butt into the gravel roadbed.

"Let's hope that's all you picked up over there…"

Lon squared his shoulders, waiting for the anticipated lecture. Trace had been on him all morning, and he was sick of it. He closed his ears to the man's ranting, relieved when he saw the thin vapor of white smoke in the distance. The sound of the steam whistle reached out to him piercing the morning air. "Hot dang," he whispered.

Brakes set, the train slid along the iron tracks, Belden matching his stride to the speed of the slowing boxcars. He left the platform, walking the length of the spur, gravel crunching beneath his boots. Lon was beside him, both of them covered hat to boot with a generous dusting of fine grained yellow-grey grit. The cows bawled a loud greeting, pink snouts poking out from the painted slats of the stock cars, the air filling with the sour smell of manure. Belden pulled off a glove and reached out to touch the nose of a curious heifer. It was warm; too warm. "Let's see what we've got," he shouted. He pulled off his hat and gave a wave to the old man in the cab of the train's engine.

The locomotive let loose with a burst of white steam, and everything disappeared behind the pale vapor as the train began to back up. Lon sprinted up the roadbed, swinging up into the cab, his arm locked elbow deep in the handrail as he leaned precariously outward watching for Trace's signals. Charlie joined them, and old man Cutter, the stockman; both taking their placed on the loading ramp, measuring the distance as the stock cars eased nearer the platform. Charlie gave Belden a high sign, his battered brown hat flopping shapelessly in the dry air, and Belden relayed the signal to Lon.

Charlie and Cutter reached out as the train ground to a halt, both men struggling with the rusted iron rod that fastened the sliding door, the metal hot with the glare of the morning sun. The bar yielded, grinding and squealing against the corroded sheath as they shoved it aside. Belden pulled himself up on to the twelve-inch planking that rimmed the edge of the narrow chute and stared into the dark interior of the first car. The Herefords were bawling insults at the invading sunlight, and they bunched and backed into the far corners. "The scours," Trace swore, "every one of them…" he could see the green, mucus-flecked streaks at their rear ends and on their hind legs.

"Well, Trace," Cutter mopped his brow with a dust-caked sleeve, "give 'em a day, maybe two, here in the pens; something to bind them up…" He continued wiping at his face, shoving more dirt into the deep lines that etched his forehead.

Belden knew the man was right, but it didn't help. "Let's get them unloaded." He grabbed a prod and climbed over the boards and into the car. Lon was beside him, weaving among the milling bovines, and together they cursed and cajoled them toward the open door. Lon slipped in a pile of fresh dung, going to his knees. He let go with a loud string of four-lettered words that exploded into the dark quiet, ending his speech with a series of ominous threats the animals seemed to understand. Trace reached out and hauled the youth to his feet. "This is what you wanted. Remember," he gestured at the retreating cattle with a wave of his arm, "all the excitement, the adventure, the glory of a trail drive?" Belden was needling the youth, reminding him of the argument they had when the boy had pleaded for permission to make the trip North.

Lon flushed, his jaws set as he wiped a soiled palm on his denims. "I slip again," he threatened, "I'll set this goddamned car on fire and barbeque your son-of-a-bitchin' cows, and to hell with the trail drive!!" He regained his footing and forced a smile as he fought his temper back under control, raising his hands in a gesture of peace. "I know, Trace. Watch my mouth," he mumbled. "I'm sorry."

They finished the unloading, Belden and his foreman inspecting the stock. Eight hundred seventy-seven head of white-faced Herefords; cows, heifers, week-old calves, and one yearling bull calf. All bawling like unweaned mavericks, still bunched as though held in the narrow confines of the railway cars. "Well, Charlie, what do you think?"

Fletcher leaned against the pole fencing. "Well, they eat good and crap regular," he nodded his silent approval, stroking his chin, watching as the cattle rooted for scraps of hay littering the floor of the pens. They were a big improvement over the gaunt longhorns they had driven up the trail from Laredo. He grinned. "They'll make a good start, Trace."

Cutter joined the pair, an anticipatory gleam in his eyes. "We still ain't settled on the price for that bull calf," he said, nodding at the small enclosure that penned the animal. He handed Trace a sheaf of papers, watching as the man scribbled his name at the bottom.

"You said a thousand, Sam," Belden reminded.

"I said maybe a thousand, depending on what the Englander was asking. Man has to make a profit, he plans on staying in this business," Cutter reminded solicitously.

"I'll buy you a drink, Sam," Belden grinned.

"Won't make the bull any less expensive." There was a faint glimmer in Cutter's eyes, a hint of a smile tugging at the corners of his wide mouth.

"A bottle," Trace returned. He had seen the man's smile. Cutter was as fond of good whiskey as he was a good haggle over prices.

Fletcher saw the exchange, a low groan escaping as he shoved back his hat. "The men, Trace," he jerked his head toward the crew. "We got a long day ahead of us…" He made a face, rolling his eyes, clutching at his throat as if dying of thirst. "If we got to stay here for two more days waitin' for your cows to get well…" He didn't finish, just flashed a lop-sided grin.

Belden considered the foreman's words. The man was right about the unplanned delay. He nodded slowly. "You get that bank draft cashed at the Wells Fargo office, Charlie," he said softly. "You get us outfitted for the trip home, and then give the men half wages." He swung his gaze to his brother and saw the grin. "Lon," he beckoned the boy to him with a long finger, intending to keep his words private. "Midnight, Lonny. I want you back at the hotel and in bed by midnight."

Lon backed away from his brother. He knew from the man's face that it would be useless to argue. Tight-lipped, he nodded his head and spun on his heel, joining the rest of the crew as they crowded around Fletcher. Someone let out a yell, the whoop picked up by the rest of the crew, culminating finally in the same eerie cry that had sent shivers up and down the back of Sherman and his blue-bellies during the War. Belden returned Fletcher's salute, watching as the men raced down the street and into the town.

******

It took two bottles of Kentucky whiskey and a five-course dinner to get Cutter to agree on the price for the bull, less money than Belden would have paid if he had foregone the haggling. He watched as Cutter staggered out of the bar and leaned back in his chair. Between the bull and the Herefords, he had laid out almost all the cash he had managed to accumulate over the past five years, and was seriously questioning his decision to get back into full time

ranching on his own. After long years of bossing outfits all
across Texas, he didn't have any real desire to settle down.
But he had wanted his son back, and that took money;
money and proof that he could give the boy a real home.

The money had been no problem. Belden's fingers
drifted to the pistol, lingering on the ivory grip. He'd spent
the last five years working for the biggest cattle company
west of the Mississippi. *Regulator*, they called him. *Range
detective*. A sardonic smile touched Belden's lips. He had
no illusions about his trade or the proper name for it. Hired
gun. In between jobs, bounty hunter. And he had been well
paid for his services. He stretched, rubbing at an ache in
his head above the eye patch.

His thoughts turned to the ranch, the spread his father
had started, the place where he and his brothers had been
born. Good grass, water; an empty house.

It was the house that troubled Belden most. Each time
he went back it was like marching again into war, one
painful memory after the other. The old man's death. His
mother. The loss of his two brothers. He tried to remember
their faces, the sounds of their voices. He couldn't. Seventeen when his mother died, he had difficulty remembering
her face; although there were times he remembered the
sound of her voice. He shook his head, thinking of how his
son had forgotten him, thinking of Elizabeth.

He wondered how many years it would take before he
could say her name and not feel the hot, searing stab deep
inside his gut. They had married young; too young, he
mused and then the War came. He poured another drink,
disappointed when the whiskey didn't help. She was
beautiful, even then, her belly big with his child, waving
goodbye to him from the front porch, her arm around Lon.
That was the picture he had kept with him, all the time he

was gone. He stroked his chin, smiling into his reflection in the puddle of spilled whiskey that was in front of him, reminding himself of what a fool he had been.

He's been gone two years; two long years. Wounded, sick with dysentery, he had been sent back to Texas, to the military hospital in Galveston. Cord Bishop was with him, his wounds less severe. *Cord Bishop*, he thought bitterly. *Commanding officer, comrade. Best friend.* The man who offered to take a message to Elizabeth at the home ranch; to give her the news he was close to home and on the mend.

He should have known when Cord came back. Would have, if he hadn't been such a trusting fool. But he would have followed Cord into Hell, through Hell, if the man had asked. And he almost had. Trace touched the patch at his eye, his fingers lingering and then raising to the white scar that sliced through his eyebrow. Instead of returning home, they returned to their War, and Cord sent him back into battle. Trace, Charlie Fletcher, and thirty raw recruits more boy than man. And only Trace and Charlie Fletcher came back. Trace blinded, his right eye gone, and Charlie's left knee shattered and stiff.

Elizabeth had left the ranch before he finally return; she and the son he had never seen. Laredo was filled with the gossip, the sordid stories that greeted him on his return. All about Cord Bishop and the woman and the bastard child she was carrying. Trace went crazy for a time, looking for them, raising Hell across a wide piece of Texas before it finally hit him that there was nothing he could do to change any of it. So he settled down to what he knew best, pushing men and cattle. He used the drives as a reason to stay on the move, returning home in the winter to lick his wounds and play big brother to Lon. Belden shifted in his chair and mouthed woman's name one more time, *Elizabeth*, shutting his good eye against the image of his son and Cord Bishop. In the eight years that had passed, he had seen the boy six times; half the agreed upon visits; and never alone.

Their last meeting had been the one three days ago. The pain of that meeting still burned deep within him.

The door to the saloon slammed open, Lon hesitating at the batwings. He let out a loud holler to announce his arrival and somehow made it through the door, the crew behind him. Charlie was with them, unsteady on his stiff leg, his face whiskey red. Trace thought of other towns, other drives, when the men on his crew would have treed a town just for the hell of it, and shook his head. Except for Lon, they were all older now, perhaps even wiser, and content to spend their money on a good meal, a friendly hand of poker or an even friendlier woman.

Lon was courting a pair of girls from the bar and stood wedged between them like a new book between a set of tarnished bookends. He allowed himself, after considerable whispered conversation, to be led towards Trace's table, not as drunk as he pretended. He untangled himself from the women and attempted a low, courtly bow. Pointing a finger at Belden, he reached out to brush away an invisible speck on the man's shoulder. "Ladies," he said, winking at his brother, "I'd like you to meet my employer." He removed his hat and bowed again. "The Archduke Wilhelm, Crown Prince of all Prussia." He straightened, a shocked look on his face, his hand going to his mouth as if he had betrayed a state secret. Eyes wide, he surveyed the room, his voice lowering in a confidential whisper. "Traveling incognito," he said, stumbling over the word, a finger pressed against his lips.

Unable to stop the grin that briefly touched his lips, he gave his brother a silent rebuke and dug into his vest pocket for his watch. He laid the piece on the table, disappointed it was only ten o'clock. Shaking his head, he stared up into his brother's face. Lon was smiling; his eyes dancing and his dark hair sweat-soaked and layered in soft curls that framed his smooth face. There was something reminiscent of a Botticelli cherub in him, an innocence that made him look even younger than his years. In a sudden stroke of compassion, Belden decided to humor him. He stood up, military straight, his shoulders back. Clicking his heels together, he made a curt bow.

The whores were properly impressed with the visiting European royalty. Belden sat down, signaling the others to do the same, not speaking. Lon addressed the two women and then turned to his brother, straight-faced as he translated, in gibberish, the giggling greetings of the ladies. Trace leaned forward and held a brief, whispered conversation with his interpreter, and then leaned back regally in his chair. He watched as Lon snapped his fingers and ordered a bottle of expensive wine. He tapped the youth's shoulder and leaned forward to whisper in his ear a second time. "*You'll pay for this, Lonny. Every dime,*" he confided, smiling at the ladies.

They were halfway through the second bottle when Belden spotted the kid. He couldn't have been more than seven or eight, a little bit of a runt with long, curly, wheat-colored hair, and he was busy swamping out the barroom. The youngster stopped his mopping, bending down in the litter to search for lost coins. Something about the boy tore at Belden, and he grabbed the bottle of wine, draining it. When he lowered the magnum, he found himself staring into the boy's solemn face.

"You a cowboy, mister?" he asked.

Belden looked the kid up and down and then put on his *get away from me* frown. If it fazed the kid, it didn't show. He just stood there across the table waiting for an answer, the mop he held in his hand a good foot taller than he was.

Trace stood up, pulling himself to his full six feet plus, the kid's head following him as he moved.

The child was pitiful. The shirt he wore was more string than cloth, and his pants must have belonged to a full-sized man. He was wearing a beat-up pair of old boots, the heels worn down to rounded nubs, and around his waist was the remainder of an old gun belt, a wooden pistol stuffed deep into the dilapidated holster. The answer Belden intended on giving the kid died unspoken. Trace cast a thoughtful look at Lonny and the two women, and then cleared his throat. "Yeah, son," he drawled. "I'm a cowboy." Lon moaned and buried his head in his arms. The two ladies shoved back their chairs, turned off their smiles, and stood up.

Belden reached out, grabbing the arm of one of the women. He knotted his fingers around her wrist, his left hand open beneath her clenched fist. The smile on his face touched everything but his eye as he increased the pressure. Her hand opened, and she dropped the watch into his outstretched palm. He let go, dismissing her with a curt nod, the watch dangling from his fingers. "Lon," he said.

Lon raised his head. He saw Trace's finger tapping the crystal on the rotating watch. "Yeah?"

"It's midnight, Lon," Belden answered. He jerked his head toward the door. "You get your butt over to the hotel. Now."

Lon pushed himself out of his chair. There was an anger in his brother's voice, an edge to his words that was uncalled for; unfair. He studied Trace's face for a time, and then turned his eyes on the small boy that was still standing beside the table. *It was the kid. There was something about the kid…* He swung his head back to his brother. "You coming?"

Belden's back stiffened at the boy's tone. "When I'm ready," he snapped. He turned from the youth, his eye searching the length of the bar. "Charlie!"

Fletcher turned his head, squinting into the dimly lit corner. He waved, acknowledging Belden's summons, and limped across the room to the table.

Trace eyed the man. "You about ready to turn in, Charlie?"

Charlie nodded, reading something in Belden's face that told him the man wanted an affirmative answer. "Yeah, Trace. I was just about to call it a night."

Belden dipped his head toward his brother. "So is Lon. But I think he's going to need some help finding the hotel."

Fletcher shrugged. "He's had the problem ever since we first hit town." He reached out and patted the boy's cheek. "C'mon, Lonny. I'll tuck you in. And if you're real good, I'll tell you a story."

Lon ducked away from the man's touch. "Go to Hell, old man!"

Charlie sighed, stepping between Belden and the youth. "I probably will," he said amicably, taking the boy's arm. "And you'll be taggin' right along with me." None too gently, he pulled the boy toward the door.

Belden watched as the pair departed, angry with the kid, even more angry with himself. He kicked a chair from in front of him and headed for the bar, intending to get drunk. "A bottle," he ordered, collaring the barkeep. Drumming his fingertips on the bar, he waited for the man. He poured a drink, and then another, emptying the glass both times in a single swallow. When his head came forward, he found himself staring into the mirror behind the bar. He could see the kid's reflection, could see that the boy was still looking at him. Picking up the glass and the bottle, he retreated to a table in the far corner of the room, irritated when the boy followed him.

It was a long night, Belden stubborn in his determination to get drunk; drunk enough to drive the knots from his stomach and the dull ache from his chest. Yet no matter how much rotgut he poured into this stomach, he remained sober. Sober enough to be aware of the boy's continued presence, the slip-slop of the kid's mop. He cursed and poured a final drink from the bottle, watching as the amber liquor washed down the sides of the container and dripped into the glass.

"Can I have a ride on your horse, mister?"

The question came with a childish boldness, catching Belden by complete surprise. He stared across the table into the kid's face and was rewarded with a smile that would have lit up the interior of a Mexican jail. "What?" Belden put down his glass and stood up, looking for the door.

"Can I have a ride on your horse," the kid repeated. His blue eyes danced and lost some of their blankness, and he jerked his head in the direction of the front exit.

Belden nodded without knowing why, and found his large hand suddenly filled with the boy's small fist. For a runt, the kid was sturdy. He led Belden out of the saloon like a grown man dragging a puppy.

Outside, the man was surprised to find the sun was just rising, the flame-bright red ball doing a fire dance across the horizon and causing pain at the back of his good eye. His stomach wasn't doing so well either, the mixture of wine and whiskey bubbling its way up his throat. The kid looked up at him knowingly. "You need some coffee, mister," he said wisely.

Belden moved aside as one of his cowhands and a lady friend passed in front of him, the top of the woman's dress still undone. He thought of the other women still inside the saloon, and shook his head in remorse. He needed a great many things right now, and coffee wasn't at the top of the list. The kid tugged at his hand again, and Belden debated the possibility of drowning him in the watering trough.

"I make real good coffee, mister," the kid said, leading the man down the boardwalk. He turned a corner and climbed a flight of stairs leading to the rooms above the saloon. He opened the door and stood aside to let Belden pass, and then scooted ahead to lead the way down the dark, narrow hallway.

The room was at the end of the corridor. Belden followed the boy across the threshold, immediately aware of the odor of sweat and cheap perfume. A big brass bed dominated one corner of the room; a small pot-bellied stove in the opposite corner. There was a speckled blue tin ware pot on the stove's single grid, and the kid disappeared just long enough to fetch water.

Belden watched as the kid built a fire, absently exploring the room. Clothes were strewn everywhere, a woman's clothes, lace and spangles and crinoline. He fingered one of the dresses, and immediately felt the boy's eyes on him. The kid lowered his head when Belden returned the look, his cheeks coloring. It was then that it occurred to the man that nowhere in the room were there any clothes or anything else that would belong to a child; nothing. "You live here?" he asked.

The boy nodded his head, brightening. "Me and my…" he paused, "…sister," he finished. He spoke again, building on the fairytale. "She keeps house for this rich lady on the other side of town. That's why she's not here." The aroma of the coffee began to fill the room. "If she was, she would fix us a good breakfast. Ham," he rubbed at his stomach, "eggs. Biscuits, too," he lied. He nodded at the bed. "You sit there, mister, and I'll bring you your coffee."

Belden sat, sinking down into the softness of quilts and feather beds, his eye on a straw pallet in the far corner behind the door. The kid brought his coffee, apologizing for the lack of milk or sugar. Cautiously, the man raised the cup to his lips.

It was good. Rich, strong; the kind of coffee made to sober a man and still his stomach. The kid stooped down, pulling off Belden's boots with an expertise that said he'd done the job many times before. Gently, he lifted the man's legs up onto the bed.

Belden lay back against the pillows, savoring the coffee and watching the kid. The boy was busy tidying up the room; putting some semblance of order to the mess. The last thing the man saw before he yielded to the need for sleep was the kid dutifully counting out the collection of pennies and other coins he had taken from his pocket, stacking them in plain sight on top of the missing woman's dresser.

CHAPTER 3

———

Belden slept until late afternoon, waking to the feel of the setting sun warm across his face. He lazed back against the pillows and watched the dust dancing in the sunlight. The room was quiet, and it took the man a little time to regain his senses and recollect how he had gotten here. The smell of cologne was in the air, and without turning over, he reached out, his hand groping at the empty spot next to him. He exhaled, momentarily disappointed. Carefully, he shifted in the bed, turning over; waiting for his stomach to catch up with the rest of his body. He saw the boy then, curled up on the straw pallet like a starved pup, a piece of old blanket in his hand. The kid was sucking his thumb.

As quietly as he could, Belden pivoted off the bed and pulled on his boots. *You got a brain in your head, Trace Belden*, he chided himself, *you'll stop this right here; right now. Just get up, get out, and never look back.* He sighed. He never had been long on brains, and was still just a tad short on common sense. Reaching up, he raked his fingers through his hair and eased the eye patch back in place. He stood up; his hands knotted at his hips, and then crossed the floor to the kid's mat. Kneeling down, he touched the boy's shoulder; keenly aware when the child tensed beneath his fingers. "I seem to remember someone asking for a ride on my horse," he said softly.

The boy stirred, hearing the man's voice. His eyes went wide, and he reacted the same as before, when the man first touched him; as if afraid he was going to be struck. Then the fire of recognition began to kindle and he relaxed. He sat up, suddenly, rubbing the sleep from his eyes. "You mean it, mister?"

"I mean it," Trace answered, reaching up to ruffle the kid's hair. His hand went back to the boy's shoulder. The youngster was nothing but skin and bones. "First we're going to get something to eat." Belden stood up and patted his stomach. "Man has to have a good meal under his belt if he expects to ride a genuine Texas cowpony," he said.

The boy's face fell. "I ain't got no money," he whispered.

Belden grabbed the kid and swung him up on his shoulders. "You can earn some." The kid ducked his head as Trace went through the door, his hands twisted tightly into the man's shirt. "I've never been in this town before," Belden lied, "and I need a guide. Someone to show me the sights, tell me the right place to get a decent meal." He felt the kid's fingers dig into his neck as he bounced down the stairway and out the door.

"That one," the boy said when they reached the board-walk. His cheek next to Belden's, he pointed down the street. "Good meat, and the eggs are really fresh!" The boy laughed, his breath warm against Belden's neck. "The cook has a mustache," he volunteered.

"So do I," Belden lowered the boy to the walkway.

"The cook's a lady!" The kid laughed again, and Belden joined in.

They ordered it all. Steak, potatoes, hot bread, and the boy put it away like he'd never sat through a decent meal and had no plans of every having one in the near future. It was a minor wonder, watching someone so small packing away so much food. He was still shoveling it in when Belden ordered a third cup of coffee.

"Looks like Charlie should have shown you the way to the hotel." Lon pulled out the chair across from Belden and sat down. He helped himself to a chunk of bread. "You get lost or something?" He took his time buttering the slice of still warm loaf.

"Or something," Belden answered. "Have you been over to Cutter's this morning?" He watched the boy's face.

Lon shook his head. He stuffed the hunk of bread into his mouth and chewed it for a long time. "I saw all of those cows I wanted to see yesterday," he said finally.

"Someday," Belden began, "half those cows are going to be yours. Might be a good idea if you remembered that."

The boy shrugged. "You can sell my half. I'd rather have the money."

Belden's fingers knotted around the edge of the table. ¡*Maldición dios*! (God damn!) he cursed silently. It was always like this when Lon had a burr in his tail. He worried it like a dog gnawing a bone, never turning loose; always ready to snap at the hand trying to take it away. "I'm going over to Cutter's place, Lon, soon as the kid is finished with his breakfast. To take a look at our cows. I expect you to come with me."

"Is he goin'?" Lon nodded at the boy.

"I promised him a ride on my horse, Lonny."

The younger Belden stood up. He stared out into the street for a long moment. "Well, I sort of promised someone a ride, too," he said, backing away from the table. "Last night, before you kicked me out of the saloon." He snapped the brim of his hat with his forefinger, the smile as sincere as his story, and headed out the door.

Angry, Trace shoved his chair away from the table. "Lon!" He was on his feet and halfway across the room before he stopped himself. Changing his mind, he went back to the counter and paid his bill, signaling for the kid to follow him.

They headed for the livery stable, the kid running along beside the man; taking two steps to Belden's one. He kept stumbling, his oversized boots flopping up and down on his feet.

Cutter was at the stable door, and he waved in greeting, his face clouding as he spied the youngster. "Hope he's with you, Trace." He shook a finger at the boy, scolding him. "Always hangin' around here, getting' in the way."

Belden ignored Cutter's grousing, his hand on the kid's shoulder. "He's with me, Sam." To the boy, he said, "You want to see my cows?"

The kid nodded his head, his eyes bright. "Yeah, Mr...."

"Belden," Trace finished. "Mr. Belden." He held out his hand like he would for a grown man. "And your name, sir?" he asked gravely.

The kid took Belden's hand in both of his, his face flushing at Cutter's loud guffaw. "Toby," he answered. His brow wrinkled and he dropped his head, chewing on the inside of his lower lip. "No last name," he muttered. "Just Toby."

"I knew a man named Noname once," Belden fibbed, as if that was what he had heard. "An Indian chief; a Cherokee. Good man," he finished. He felt the kid's hand tighten in his. "Come on, Mr. Noname. We'll go look at those cows."

The boy followed after Belden, climbing up on the fence as the man pointed out the Herefords, dutifully nodding his head as Belden extolled the traits that made the animals such desirable meat stock. The kid proved a good listener, and Belden noted that he had the same gleam in his eyes that he himself saw staring from his own mirror every time he shaved.

"Who's that?" Toby rose up on his toes and pointed to the far pen where the Hereford bull calf was corralled.

"Solomon," Cutter answered. He joined the pair at the fence, a piece of straw between his teeth.

"Solomon?" Belden repeated, studying the man.

"Sure," Cutter answered, his watery eyes squinted against the bright sun. "Just like in the Bible." He swung his gaze to Toby, paying no attention to Belden's shaking head.

"Who was Solomon?" the kid asked, his eyes on the yearling.

"Why, he was a king," Cutter replied before Belden could answer, the same gleam in his eye as when he was horse-trading. "A wise king."

The boy's eyes narrowed. "Is he wise, Mr. Belden?" he asked, pointing at the Hereford.

Belden shot a menacing glance at Cutter. There was no animal as contrary or as stupid on God's green earth as a bovine. *Unless it was an old man intent on hurrahing a small boy.* "Not really, Toby," he answered.

Cutter laughed. "No, he ain't wise, boy!" His voice lowered and he put an arm around the boy's shoulder. "I call him Solomon because of all the wives and concubines he's got; all the babies he's going to have." He clapped the boy's back and gave him a quick hug.

"He can have babies?" the boy whispered, pressing his face closer to the fence.

Cutter laughed again, slapping his knees. "Sweet Jesus, no, child!" he chortled. "He *makes* babies!!"

Belden pushed his way past the old man, pulling the kid down from the fence. "He better, old man," he said

pointedly, his good eye narrowing. He turned back to the
boy. "We're going for the ride, Toby. Right now." He ush-
ered the boy into the stable, the sound of Cutter's laughter
fading behind him as he led the way to the back stalls.

The bay lifted its head and snorted in greeting. Toby
reached through the slats, his fingers stroking the soft black
muzzle. "What's his name, Mr. Belden?"

Trace had to think about that awhile. Since acquiring
the gelding, he had given the animal a variety of names,
none of which bore repeating in front of the youngster.
"I call him the Brown Bast….," he caught himself, "the
Brown Beast," he finished. Avoiding the kid's eyes, he slid
the retaining poles aside and collected his gear off the side
railing. The kid started asking questions again, a hundred
of them in the time it took to saddle the horse. *Where was
he born? How old is he? Why do you have to poke him in the
belly with your knee? How fast can he go?* And, thinking
of Solomon, *can he make babies, too?* Belden reached out,
clapping his hand over the kid's mouth, and hoisted him
into the saddle. He pulled up behind the boy and nudged
the gelding in the sides, the horse humping its back at the
additional weight before moving out at a slow walk.

They rode for hours, the bay dropping into his rocking
chair run, eating up the miles with the pure joy of running.
The kid was pressed against Belden's belly, both hands
locked around the saddle horn, and for the first time since
the man had met him, speechless. It was only when they
headed back into town that the magic left the boy. He
heaved a big sigh and rested his head on Belden's chest,
silent in a different way.

It was late when they returned to the town, and they
spent even longer in the stable, the boy brushing the gelding until the bay's hide took on the smooth shine of pol-

ished mahogany and all the snarls were worked out of his black mane and tail. The horse took it in stride, relishing the attention. He stretched his neck, pulling his lips open in what seemed a smile as he leaned into the brush. Trace reached out, tapping the kid's shoulder. "Your sister will be worried about you, Toby."

"She's not my sister," the boy replied. He pressed his head into the bay's long mane and was silent again. "She just has me say that, so her friends…" his voice trailed off, and his shoulders sagged. It was obvious that the boy was sobbing; trying hard to conceal the tears.

Belden had taken some long walks in his life, but the one going back to Clancy's bordello was the longest. He dragged it out as long as he could, stopping for a late supper when he spotted the crew gathered at one of the cafes. This time the kid didn't eat so much, his face shining as he listened to the loud bantering between the men. He leaned back, listening to their tall stories, and before anyone realized what was happening, fell asleep in his chair.

Gently, Belden picked him up, waiting as Charlie held the door open for him. He carried him down the street, the boy's breath coming in warm even gasps against his chest. He was light, too damn light. Belden started up the stairs, filled with a building resentment for a woman he had never met. And he did want to meet her. Just one time.

The hallway was dark, a single lantern burning, the glass caked with black soot. The door to the kid's room was closed, a narrow shaft of soft yellow light coming from beneath. Belden could hear the sound of voices. He pressed his ear against the door and heard laughter, the soft lilt of a woman, and the heavier baritone of a man's. Cursing, he cupped his hand over the boy's ear, pulling his head tighter to his chest. He tapped on the door with the toe of his boot. Hard.

The door opened a small crack and the woman peered out, silhouetted by the lantern light at her back. She was far from plain looking, with blond, curly hair like her son's. Her dress was a deep blue, low cut, the ripe breasts straining invitingly against the bodice. She was, Belden thought, surprisingly young. *Except for the eyes.* They were blue, like the boy's, but filled with the ruthlessness that comes with premature age, and the emptiness of no longer knowing how to care. Belden's gaze shifted away from her face, slowly drifting down her body. *Any other time*, he mused, *any other place…* He shook the thought from his mind, the boy suddenly heavy in his arms. "I brought your son home," he said, lifting the boy away from his chest.

The woman stepped quickly into the hallway, pulling the door shut behind her, her hand on the knob. "You'll have to take him downstairs," she hissed, visibly annoyed. "To the supply room." When Belden didn't move, she lifted her eyes to his face, angry. "I have a caller. A gentleman caller!!"

Belden remained still, standing his ground like some dumb dirt farmer, the boy snuggled in his arms. He nodded at Toby. "He's sleeping *here*," he declared. He kicked the door open and shoved his way past the woman.

"*What the …!?*"The man on the bed stood up, grabbing his pants. A wine bottle fell from the table beside the bed and rolled across the uneven floor in an erratic circle. "I paid for this room! Twenty dollars!"

Belden smiled from the darkness of the doorway, filled with an urgent need to laugh. "Fine," he said. He nodded at the pallet in the far corner. "You and the *lady*," he made the word sound obscene, "can share the kid's bed, Cord." He crossed the room to the brass bedstead and laid the boy down.

Bishop's eyes narrowed and he struggled to his feet, his hand groping for the lantern on the table beside the bed. He lifted it slowly, the shaded glass revealing Belden's pant legs, his gun belt, the front of his shirt, and finally, his face. The man staggered back against the bed. He recovered, the liquor firing him with a bravado meant to impress the woman. He lay a sweaty palm on Belden's shoulder. "You get that little bastard out of here," he breathed.

Belden hit him, planting a doubled fist in the middle of Bishop's soft belly. The second blow was aimed six inches lower. Trace caught him as he fell forward, his left hand stifling the man's cry. Straining to hold Bishop erect, he dug into his own pocket and withdrew a gold piece. He shoved the coin into the man's hand. "Find another room, Cord," he advised. He changed his mind. "*I'll* help you find another room." His arm closed around the man's neck, and he dragged him toward the door.

Bishop fought the abduction, his fingers groping for the door frame, Belden's hand still covering his mouth. Eyes wide, he silently begged the woman's help, his muffled outcries growing fainter as he was pulled into the dark hallway.

Belden hauled the man along the narrow passageway. The room to his right was empty, its door open wide. Trace shoved the man inside, pinning him against the papered wall.

Five long months in a Union prison camp had taught Belden well. He remembered all the beatings, the long black nights when he was dragged from his cell and questioned. Over and over again; all the questions. And when he refused to answer, the endless rain of gloved fists. They had stuffed his mouth with the filthy remnants of his own clothing and then took turns beating him. Again and again. Once, he fought back.

It cost him his eye.

Belden felt the dead weight of Bishop's body in his arms, the sensation of warm blood on his fist jolting him back to the reality of the here and now. Shoulders aching, he eased the man down to the floor. Bishop was no good to him dead. His hatred for Bishop had kept him alive in prison, and later gave him the will to fight death the long torturous weeks he lay in the hospital. It was his need to get even with Bishop and the woman that had given him the will to go on. He reached out, fingering the man's fleshy neck, probing for a pulse. Relieved, he sat back on his heels. "Not yet, Cord," he whispered, rising. "Not all at once." He shook his head. He wanted Bishop to die in small bits and pieces, a little at a time. The same way he had died when Bishop and the woman had taken his son.

The hallway was empty when Belden stepped back out into the dim light. He took a series of deep breaths, his head clearing, and the sweat at his back and arm pits growing cold. His fists hurt, and he extended his arms, studying the backs of his hands. The knuckles were swollen; blue-white, flecks of blood and spittle streaking the scraped flesh. He wiped the back of his hands on his pants leg and started down the corridor to the woman's room.

She was waiting for him, sitting on the edge of the bed, an ivory colored dressing gown covering her arms and shoulders. The robe was held in place by a single button and a narrow sash, her legs exposed up to her thighs. A smile played on the pale lips, and she was toying with the collar, her fingernails tracing thin pink lines on her near naked breasts.

Belden turned and jerked the door wide open. "Your friend is in the room across the hall," he said coldly.

The bedsprings sang as the woman stood up. "I don't think I'll be able to help him now," she smiled, her voice a lilting, singsong. She opened her gown, her back to the bed.

"Get out," Belden rasped. He jerked his head toward the hallway. She left, reluctantly, her hand trailing across his cheek.

Toby stirred and whimpered, the bed creaking as he shifted. Belden strode across the room. Amazingly, the kid was asleep, his body barely making an impression on the thick covers as he curled into a tight ball. Trace rolled the boy over onto this back and undressed him, right down to the pair of pinned-together long johns, and not once did the child move. Cursing, Belden crawled in beside him, the anger he felt at the woman's indifference clawing at his belly like a raking spur.

CHAPTER 4

———

"How many?" Belden stood beside Charlie Fletcher, his hat pulled down low on his forehead.

"So far, about twenty head." Fletcher chewed thoughtfully on the stub of a burnt-out cigar. "I've got Cully, Poke and Delgado still working through the others…"

"Damn!" Belden lifted his gloved hands from the fence rail, and then slapped them back down. "*Damn!*" He eyed the milling Herefords, anxious. "We'll need some kerosene; a couple of sprinkling cans." The thought of treating the animals riled him, and he cursed again.

Fletcher was drawing circles in the dirt with the toe of his boot, reflective. "Thought at first, maybe it was just scrapes and tears from shipping." He lifted his shoulders in resignation. "It ain't the end of the world, Trace. A couple of cows with the mange."

"It is if we don't get it stopped." Belden was disgusted. It struck him all at once, how different it was when the cattle were his. Not that he would have fretted any less about another man's stock. It was just that, somehow, this was different. He turned away from the fence and stared back down the long row of pens, watching as Cully hazed two more animals into the middle passageway. Shaking his head, he mounted the bay. "I'll get the things we need from Cutter," he said. "Lonny!" Shading his good eye, he stood up in the stirrups and called for his brother.

They rode the short distance from the pens to Cutter's store, keeping the horses at a slow walk. Lon took his hat off and mopped his forehead with his shirt sleeve. "Where's your shadow?" He wiped at the sweatband with his elbow, rotating the hat. When he set the hat back on his head, the wide brim hid his eyes.

Belden exhaled, recognizing the boy's tone. "I don't know, Lonny," he answered truthfully.

"Yeah?" The man's answer wasn't enough, and the boy kept on. "It's been two days, and the brat hasn't missed having at least one meal with you." The sarcasm in Lon's voice was increasing. "Thought maybe you were going to take him to raise," he pulled the sorrel to a halt and, lifting his right leg up and over the saddle horn, slipped off the mare's back. "He's about the right age, almost the same size as Adam. Maybe you could…"

"Shut up!" Belden dismounted and wrapped the bay's reins around the hitching rail, pulling the knot tight with a savage jerk. He reached out to his brother. "I mean it, Lon…"

The youth pulled away, his lips tight as he stared past his brother. "Well, ain't that a surprise," he mocked, shaking his head.

Belden turned, following his brother's gaze. Toby was on the front porch, a heavy can of kerosene in his hands. "Mr. Cutter said you'd be coming for this." He tried to lift the container, his knuckles white against the wire handle, the grin he wore threatening to go all the way around his head.

"You go get the sprinkling cans, Lonny," the man

ordered. He climbed the stairs, reaching out to help the smaller boy with his burden. "Mornin', Toby."

"Mr. Cutter says your cows got the mange." Toby followed alongside Belden as the man went into the mercantile, his hand still on the pail handle. "He says that if all the cows get it, you'll have to shoot 'em. He says…"

"Mr. Cutter says too much, Toby." Belden placed his hand on the boy's shoulder. The anger that was building in him put an edge on his words that took the smile from the boy's face. Chagrined, Belden turned his touch into a reassuring pat, coaxing the grin back. "You want to help?" he asked.

"Sure!' The smile came as quickly as it had faded, the blue eyes lighting.

"Then go give Lon a hand," he said, giving him a gentle shove.

"Trace."

Belding turned, facing the voice. "Linc," he greeted.

The lawman was at the counter, his elbows resting on the glass-topped case. He chewed at his tobacco, watching as Lon and Toby wrangled over who would carry what, his eyes working the interior of the store with a ferret-like thoroughness. "Saw Cord," he ventured, his gaze back on the two boys.

Belden was beside the man, his fingers busy with a dark-papered cheroot. "Cows got a bit of a problem," he lifted his index finger to the corner of his mouth, picking at a stray piece of tobacco. He clenched the cigar between his teeth and lit up, sucking deeply.

McLane nodded absently. "Lot of sickness going around this time of year. Accidents, too." He studied Belden's profile in a soot-caked mirror. There was no change in the man's face, Belden concentrating on his smoke. "Seems Cord took a fall," he shook his head in sympathy. "A bad fall," he finished.

Belden stared through a thin haze of smoke, his good eye watering. "Seems Cord should watch where he steps," he said solemnly. "A man could get killed, being in the wrong place at the wrong time."

"Well, he told Doc he doesn't plan on havin' another accident. Not like this one." McLane reached out, toying with a piece of yard goods at his elbow. He rubbed the fabric between his thumb and forefinger, thoughtful. "He seemed put out some. Almost like somebody pushed him."

Belden's eyebrow arched, and his forehead wrinkled as if he were expending a great deal of effort in deep thought. He shook his head slowly. "Can't believe Cord would have any enemies. Not in his own town." He took another long drag on the cigar, rolling the smoke around in his mouth before exhaling through his nose.

"You plan on leaving here soon, Trace?" McLane was tiring of the game, and the weariness was in his voice.

"Soon as my cows are fit for the trail," the other answered.

The lawman pushed himself away from the counter, helping himself to a cracker from the open barrel. "I want to get you them healthy, Trace. Soon." There was a gnawing deep down inside McLane's belly, and his stomach rumbled loudly.

Belden nodded, understanding the man's suggestion. "I don't like being here any more than you like having me," he said dryly. He chewed on the cigar, grinning at the man. "You tell Cord I hope he doesn't take any more falls," he lied.

Disgusted, McLane swore under his breath, his face coloring as Mrs. Cutter flushed and turned her head. He strode from the store, his boots thumping loud across the plank flooring.

"Lon says he's ready," Toby reached up, tugging at Belden's sleeve. He pointed to the open door.

Trace nodded, his gaze still on the departing lawman. He grabbed the boy's hand and led him out the door, grabbing the gunny sack full of sprinkling cans. Lon was waiting for him, the can of kerosene strapped securely to his saddle. He watched as his older brother hefted the boy up onto the bay. "McLane went by me cussin' up a blue streak. What'd he want?"

Belden knotted the gunny sack in place next to Toby's knee. He pulled up behind the saddle, settling himself evenly on the gelding's broad back. "Linc is just doing his job," he said, swinging the bay away from the hitching rail. He knew why McLane had come looking for him. The lawman hadn't swallowed Bishop's story about a fall, any more than he would have in McLane's place.

"He told you to get out of town," Lon said contemptuously.

"He told me to get my cows healthy," Belton declared. "And that's just what I figure on doing." He shot an ominous glance at his brother that stilled the boy's attempted retort.

Sullen, Lon turned away from Trace, his eyes straight ahead. McLane was backing Trace into a corner, pushing him. Ordering him to leave town like some no name saddle tramp. It didn't matter how the lawman had worded it; the meaning was the same. And Trace was going to turn tail and run. "What about Adam?" he asked, swinging his head toward the older man.

"What about him?" Belden had long ago learned the advantage of answering an unwanted question with a question. It gave him more time to work a thing over in his mind, to prepare an answer.

"You're going to let Bishop and the woman have him! Just ride out of here..." Lon's face was red, and his voice was growing louder.

"I'm going to take care of my own business," Belden growled. "It would be a good idea if you did the same."

Toby was oblivious to the tension between the two, his interest centered on the slatted pens. Charlie Fletcher and the other hands were still culling the herd, the air alive with the jingle of curb chains and silver dollar-sized spurs. The yellow dust in the pens lay thick atop the packed earth, rising in man-made dust devils as a man would spot another diseased Hereford and separate the reluctant cow out from the others. Toby watched, sucking in a bellyful of air as one of the cowpony's cut a sharp circle and leaned precariously sideways, the rider seeming to hang suspended from some unseen strings until the horse righted itself and man and animal became one again.

"Charlie!" Belden shouted above the noise from the pens, his arm lifted. He signaled for the man to join him and dismounted, ground-hitching the bay at the fence.

"About thirty head, Trace," Fletcher dismounted, answering the man's unspoken question. "Mostly full growed cows; one or two heifers." He reached down, rubbing at the ache in his gimpy leg.

Trace nodded. He slapped his hand against the gunny sack. "Cutter only had three cans." The bay snorted and laid its ears back as the man's hand thumped against the bag of galvanized cans. Belden reached up, grabbing Toby's leg as the boy instinctively gripped the gelding's sides with his knees. "He does that, and you jab him in the ribs that way, he's going to dump you on the ground," he cautioned. He lifted the boy down from the saddle and turned back to Fletcher. "You, me and Lonny," he said finally. "We'll run them through the chutes in threes; sprinkle them down good, then keep 'em away from the others."

Fletcher stroked the day-old stubble at his chin. "Going to put us further behind, Trace. We've been pushin' it as it is." He nodded toward the southern horizon, thinking of the coming spring and the seasonal rains.

"We've had two dry springs in a row, Charlie, and a mild winter." Belden reached out, taking Lon's reins when the boy dismounted. He tied the lines around the fence, watching as the boy unstrapped the can of kerosene. Tapping Toby on the shoulder, he unfastened the gunny sack and put it in the boy's hands and then gave him a shove in Lon's direction.

Charlie nodded, his eyes narrowing. "Mild winter here, like always," he reasoned, pointing a gloved hand at the flat landscape beyond the town. "But we're gettin' closer to spring comin'," he swept the horizon with his arm. "I've been watchin' the sky. Won't be all that long before the rains start fallin' here, and we'll be gettin' the same in the hill country. We don't get on the trail soon, we're gonna see the worst of it before we get back home." There was something forbidding in his face, as if he were fighting an unpleasant memory. "We got rivers to cross on the way home, Trace, and …"

Belden grimaced. "You're borrowing trouble, Charlie," he interrupted.

Embarrassed, the foreman kicked at a dried pile of cow chips. "Yeah," he admitted. "Maybe I am. It's an old habit. If I ain't worryin' about the cows, I'm worryin' about the weather."

"And your sore knee, and the men, and the food, and how good a green-back dollar is," Trace joshed, grinning at the man.

"*Yankee* dollar," the other corrected. He stuffed his hands into his hip pockets. "We ain't gettin' no cows treated, standin' here jawin'." He turned his back on Belden and headed down the row of pens. "Cully!" he roared.

Belden headed for the far holding pen, watching as Charlie gathered the crew around him and began issuing orders. Lon and Toby were at the chute, the sound of the arguing reaching out to the man.

"You just keep out of my way, brat," Lon warned. He took a jab at the boy with his free hand, forcing him away from the fence. "Far away," he finished. He tipped up the container of kerosene, filling the last sprinkling can.

Belden reached out, catching Toby as the boy backed up into him. "I've got just the job for you, Toby," he said. He pointed to a stair-step pile of baled hay. "You get up there; make a count, tell me how many animals have the mange." He watched as the boy worked his way up to the top-most bale.

Lon was standing at the fence, laughing. There was a taunting sound to his laughter, and it reached out to the smaller boy. Lon shoved back his hat and put his thumb to his nose, waggling his fingers. Toby pouted, and the answered the gesture with a signal of his own, one rigid finger rising skyward. Lon's smile turned upside down. "You little bastard..."

Trace reached out, hauling Lon back as he lunged toward the stack of hay. "We've got cows to take care of, Lonny," he reminded. He nodded toward the string of kerosene-filled sprinkling cans.

They started the cattle through the chute, Fletcher joining Belden and Lon on the narrow plank walkway that surrounded the rail fence. Balancing himself, Charlie stepped across the narrow pathway, teetering on the opposite railing as he straddled the chute. Puffing, he lowered himself down onto the walkway opposite Belden. Three bawling Herefords were prodded into the narrow shaft, Belden reaching out as the first animal came to him. He covered the animal's nose with his gloved hand, using the other to apply the kerosene. The cow bellowed and tried to back up, then lunged forward, eyes rolling as the kerosene penetrated the open scabs. In turn, they dosed each of the diseased Herefords, cursing as the liquid slopped on their clothes. Lon kicked at the last heifer, urging her through the passageway, swearing as the animal shook like a wet dog and showered him with the excess fuel.

Fletcher clambered up the fence, slipping as he put his weight on his lame leg. He swung down, pulling off his oil-soaked gloves. "They're cryin' like spanked babies," he said, wiping a sleeve across his mouth.

Belden nodded, spitting into the dirt. The smell of the kerosene was all around them, the thin oil permeating their clothing, burning their skin. "We'll dose them again tomorrow." He rubbed his tongue across his lips, tasting the shale oil. "I got to get out of these clothes, get a bath!" Turning, he started toward the other pens. "You get one of the other hands to clean this up, put the cans away…"

Fletcher was beside him, feeling the itching; the slow burn as the kerosene-soaked denim chafed his skin. "I'm going to crawl into a tub with these on," he lifted his wet shirt away from his belly, "hire some girl to scrub my back and my shirt at the same time."

Belden laughed, the sound stopping suddenly. He reached out his hand and pulled Fletcher to a halt. "My God," he breathed, the color draining from his face.

Charlie half-turned, following Belden's gaze, his own face going ash grey. Lon was beside the watering trough, his head bent, one hand covering his face as he started to light a smoke.

The boy scratched his thumbnail over the sulfur-tipped match, cursing when the stick failed to ignite. He tried a second time, flinging the match to the ground, awestruck as a blue flame shot down his thumb. The fire flickered briefly in the light breeze, and then flared up again, hungrily licking its way back down the boy's kerosene covered hand toward the cuff of his chambray shirt.

"Lonny!" Belden broke into a run, charging across the feedlot, his feet threatening to disobey his urgent commands. He could see the panic in Lon's face, the boy frozen where he stood. The fire was growing, following the grimy trail where the kerosene had soaked into the boy's sleeves. Lon backed up, as if he thought he could back away from the fire. And then he started to run.

Trace threw himself forward, lunging across the watering trough, his shoulder crashing into the boy's ribs. He pulled the youth down into the dirt and felt the heat of his own shirt as it ignited. Fighting his own fear, he struggled to hold the boy. They rolled over, twice, and then Belden pulled the kid to his feet. He dumped him into the watering trough, clambering in after him and forcing him to the bottom. The water closed over their heads, smothering the flames. Lon struggled against his brother's grasp, swallowing a mouthful of brackish water as he gasped desperately for air.

They stood up in unison, Belden's hands still wound in the boy's sleeves, the water rolling off their charred clothing. Fear, more than anger, prompted the man's reaction. He dug his fingers into the boy's arms, shaking him hard. "What the hell is the matter with you!?" he roared.

"Trace!" Fletcher grabbed Belden's shoulder. "*Trace!!*" Carefully, he reached out, prying the man's fingers loose from the boy's arms.

Belden lifted both hands away from Lon's shoulders, silently willing his pounding heart to a more normal beat. "You all right, Lonny?" he asked, the subsiding fear making the words brittle. He reached out, picking at the remainder of the boy's right shirt sleeve, pulling the frayed blue-black threads away from the reddened skin. He closed his good eye, thinking of the thing that could have happened. "We'll the find the doctor," he said, still fighting the panic, his mouth dry, "have him take a look at this."

"I'm all right!" Lon's face had regained some it its coloring. He stepped out of the water, mindful of the gathering hired hands. He could feel their eyes on him, knew they had been watching. Had seen him run scared like some greenhorn, just as they had seen Trace shake him almost senseless. He felt his brother's hand on his shoulder again, and jerked away. "*I said I was all right!!*" he raged.

"You're coming with me to the Doc's," Trace said firmly. He took the boy's arm, ushering him toward the main street. Toby fell in behind them, his face white, stopping when Belden waved him away.

******

Trace stood up and stretched; his arms and legs numb. Noiselessly, he padded across the floor, pausing at the window to peer out into the street. The sound of Lon's breathing reached out to him, and he turned back to the bed, his hands closing around the brass frame.

The boy's right arm was swathed in a gauze bandage, traces of red showing on the back of his fingers and at his shoulder. He shifted in the bed, groaning, and his brow knotting as he attempted to roll over onto his stomach. Without waking, he eased onto his back, settling deeper into the bunched pillows. His breathing became more regular once again, and his face smoothed into a lineless tranquility.

Trace studied the youth's face for a long time. The horror of what had almost happened still gripped him, gnawing at his very soul. He was torn apart by his feelings. There was a deep gratitude for the boy's well-being and an almost deeper rage at his stupidity. *A cigarette*, Belden fumed. *A lousy cigarette*! His grip on the bed frame increased. It had been a mistake, bringing Lonny along. The kid was too green, too irresponsible. And his moods. They were enough to drive a saint to mortal sin. A man had to watch everything he said, everything he did. It was worse than being under the eye of God.

He moved away from the bed, going back to the window, wishing for a drink and cursing his desire for a smoke. His eye explored the dark porches of the shuttered stores, drifting finally to the light-filled gaps that marked the entrances to the saloons. He sighed. Fletcher and the men would be in the beer halls, making the rounds. Wine. Women.

Women. That single thought riled Belden even more. Between Toby and Lon, his opportunities to visit the bawdy houses were limited. He swore bitterly. He could have done better staying at home in Laredo; relishing the monthly visits to town, and it would have been a lot simpler.

The door to the adjoining room opened and then slipped quietly shut, the sound of a man tiptoeing across the floor prompting Belden to back into the darkness at the corner of the room. Without thinking, he fingered the butt of his revolver.

"Trace?" Charlie Fletcher appeared, framed in the light, a bottle in his outstretched hand.

Belden stepped out of the shadows at the foot of the bed. "Charlie," he greeted, his voice a soft whisper. He put a finger to his lips and nodded at the bed, and then moved to the doorway. He stooped down to pick up his boots, and then gestured to the other room, pulling the door shut.

"He all right?" Charlie worked the cork free from the whiskey bottle he had commandeered from the saloon, and passed it to the man.

Belden took a long drink before nodding his head. He wiped his wet lips with the back of his hand, his voice whiskey hoarse. "Doc gave him something to make him sleep; said he'd be out until morning."

Charlie nodded and held out his hand for the bottle. "Thought so." He took a swig. "How bad?" he asked.

Trace shook his head, rolling his shoulders in an attempt to ease the ache between them. "Not as bad as it looks. Doc says a day or so in bed, he'll be fine."

"Fine enough to have his butt beat?" Fletcher rarely wasted words when strong sentiment moved him. "My God, Trace," he faced the man, returning the bottle. "Can you imagine the hell we would have had if he had lit up in the pens?"

Coming from any other man, the reference to the boy's carelessness would have evoked a strong response from Belden. As it was, there was a hint of ice in his words. "I'll straighten him out when he's on his feet, Charlie," he promised.

Fletcher chose to ignore the chill in Belden's voice. "You better." He jerked his head toward the outer door. "Toby's downstairs. Been hauntin' the place ever since you brought Lonny back from Doc's. Said to tell you there were twenty-seven."

The reference to the number puzzled Belden, making him scratch his head. The smile came, slowly. "I told him to count the cows. When we were dosing them."

Charlie nodded. He wriggled a finger, pointing at the bottle Belden was hoarding. "I figured you might want to get out for a while; stretch your legs," he said lamely.

Trace grinned across at the man. "It isn't my legs that's been giving me a problem." *What's between them*, he though dryly. "What about Toby?"

"Send him on up. I'll put him to bed, he gives me any sass." Fletcher settled into the chair beside the bed, the bottle between his palms. He watched as Belden pulled on his boots.

Trace grabbed his hat, grateful for the reprieve. "You need me, Charlie..."

"I'll have someone kick down the door of the nearest whorehouse," Fletcher joked. He tossed his hat on the bed and waved the man away. "Stay away from the little redhead," he cautioned. "Cully says if you bed her, you're going to remember it for a long time." He pointed to his crotch.

Belden paused, his hand on the doorknob. "He find that out *before* he slept with her, or after?"

Charlie laughed. "He's young. He bedded her, and then asked why she wasn't workin' steady."

The whiskey was working on Belden, warming his insides. "Where's Cully now?" he asked, a smile crawling across his face.

Fletcher recognized the gleam in Belden's good eye. "He's at Clancy's," he answered. "Why?"

Trace's smile had grown. "Bishop has been visiting a whore at Clancy's. Regular. I thought I'd stake Cully to a free tumble with the lady."

"You vindictive bastard!" Fletcher reached over to the bed and picked up a pillow. He heaved the missile at Belden's head, laughing.

"It was just a thought." Belden ducked, and retreated through the door. He could still hear Charlie's laughter as he headed down the stairs.

CHAPTER 5

———

Belden roused from a troubled sleep, the faint smell of burning kerosene teasing his nostrils. Fully awake, he punched at his pillow, cursing the dream that brought the cold sweat at his forehead and back. He sat up on the side of the bed, his head clearing, and felt a chill sweep across his shoulders. *Damned weather*, he cursed. *Sweat the tallow off you during the day, and freeze your ass at night.* Cautiously, he rose from the bed, easing the springs up as he moved. Still they squeaked their song into the black quiet. Mouthing another silent curse, he paused, his eyes on the bed across from him. Lon was still asleep, his chest rising and falling evenly. Satisfied, Trace crossed the room to the window, the dream still haunting him. He could see Lon on fire, only this time there was no watering trough. The acrid scent of kerosene came again, just as he had smelled it when he and Lon were rolling on the ground.

He gripped the window sash with both hands and prepared to shut the window. The odor was stronger now, heavy on the night air. Only this time, it wasn't any dream. Trace stuck his head out the window, his naked back white under the full moon. There was a bright orange glow fringing the darkness at the end of the street, and the pained sounds of cattle bawling.

Abruptly, he pulled his head in the window, grabbing his pants as he headed for the door, his belt and holster looped over his arm. Storming into the outer room, he punched a leg into the stiff denim. "Charlie!"

Fletcher bolted upright from his bed, his feet hitting the floor with a bone-shaking thud. "Sweet Jesus!" He saw the urgency in Belden's face and said no more, reaching for his own pants.

Bare-footed the two men pounded down the boardwalk, a trail of 'punchers in varying states of undress falling in behind them. Lincoln McLane appeared out of the darkness, almost colliding with Belden, his carbine crooked in his right arm. Somewhere in the distance, a bell began a frantic clanging.

They reached the pens just as the first of the doctored Herefords broke through, the sound of tearing wood almost obliterated by the crackling noise of burning flesh. Trace flung out his arm, grimacing as Charlie collided with his elbow. Both men jumped aside, a flaming cow tearing past them. Belden could feel the heat of the fire on his face, and was sickened at the stench of burning hair. One by one, the frenzied Herefords stampeded into the street, the dry fence railings beginning to smolder as the burning cows hung up side-by-side in the splintered slats. They bunched at the opening, one cow igniting another, and another. The town came alive with the glowing orange flame of living lanterns, the crazed animals charging blindly down the streets and into the alleyways.

Belden grabbed his men as they raced by him, issuing terse orders. Fletcher zigzagged his way among the cows in his hobbling run, heading for the livery. When he reappeared, he had three horses behind him, and two men waiting to lace the saddles.

"God, Trace," McLane surveyed the pandemonium. He levered a shell into his rifle.

Belden nodded without answering, unholstering his revolver. Cocking the weapon, he took aim at a charging cow, discharging the pistol point blank. The animal folded up and fell to its knees, keeling over on to its side. He moved in as close as he could and made the killing shot.

It was grisly work. Lon joined them, his pale face haggard and drawn in the flickering firelight. McLane sent him back to his office with the key to the gun rack. When the youth returned, he was carrying three rifles, and they went through the streets in a ragged line, dispatching the burning cows; amazed at the distance some of the animals had traveled. It was dawn before they finished. They made the count, weaving in and out among the scattered string of still smoldering corpses. Belden knelt on one knee beside the last animal. "Twenty-seven," he breathed. He pulled himself erect, his face gaunt.

Fletcher pulled up beside them, hesitant as he appraised McLane. Then, not caring, he flung something solid to the ground. "A torch, Trace," he said, his mouth dry. "I found another one at the pens."

"My god," McLane mumbled. His chest rose and fell, the skin under his right eye twitching. He swung his eyes back to Belden.

"The men know?" Trace asked, ignoring the lawman's careful scrutiny.

"Just me and Cully," came the answer. Fletcher cut his eyes at Lon. "And the kid."

Belden nodded. "It's been a long night," he said finally. He stared down at his grime-caked, soot blackened feet.

"Get the men some breakfast, Charlie." Absently, he lifted his head. "The rest of the cows…?"

"Didn't lose any," Fletcher answered. He rubbed at the growing soreness in his left leg. "I left a couple of men at the stock pens. Might be a good idea if we do that for a time."

"Yeah," Belden agreed. He handed McLane the borrowed rifle and indicated for Lon to do the same. "Thanks for the loan, Linc. And the help."

McLane took the weapons, not liking the man's demeanor. Belden was quiet; too quiet. He could see something working behind that damned solitary eye, and it was something the lawman didn't like. "Trace," he began. It was like talking to a great stone wall. Disgusted, the lawman turned on his heel and stalked down the street.

"What now?" Lon was uncomfortably close to Trace's right shoulder.

"We go back to the hotel and get you cleaned up." He was giving the boy the once over. "We're going to need to change those bandages, Lonny."

Lon had to dogtrot to keep up with his brother's lengthening stride. "But what about the torches, about what Charlie…"

"I'll take care of it," Trace said quietly. *I'll damned sure take care of it*, he promised silently.

******

McLane watched from the front porch of the jail, noting the grim silence of Belden's crew as the men dragged the charred carcasses from the street. It was slow work, and they went about the task methodically. Two men, mounted, one carcass. The streets were crisscrossed with rows of wide, shallow furrows.

The lawman pushed himself away from the brick wall, his eyes narrowing. Belden had come out of the hotel. He was dressed for the trail; clean denims, a light blue work shirt, a leather vest hanging loose on his broad shoulders. He paused on the boardwalk, cupping his hand against the breeze as he struggled to light a white-papered cigarette. The smoke clenched firmly between set lips, he reached up, adjusting his Stetson; that move followed by something McLane had seen many times in the past. Belden's hands dropped to his waist, checking his gun belt, and then he moved on. McLane sighed, and went back inside his office. When the reappeared, he was carrying his rifle. Belden was gone.

McLane hurried along the boardwalk, shouldering his way through the crowd of sidewalk cowboys supervising the removal of the dead Herefords. Cursing, his shoved his way through the knot of men, ignoring their indignant responses. His stride lengthening, he crossed the street, heading directly for the branch of the Galveston bank Bishop managed.

Belden was inside. He leaned across Bishop's desk, his fingers toying with the man's tie. "Three thousand, Cord. For twenty-seven Herefords, and pay for my crew."

"You're crazy!!" Bishop leaned back in his chair, trying to escape Belden's probing fingers. The move came too late.

Belden flicked his wrist, knotting the man's tie around his clenched fist. He jerked the man toward him, lifting him out his chair. The pistol was already in his right hand, and he placed the cold barrel close to Bishop's bobbing Adam's apple. "Not as crazy as you, Cord, if you think you aren't going to pay," he whispered.

McLane eased through the door, leaving it ajar. "Put it up, Trace," he ordered, levering a cartridge into the rifle's chamber. There was a loud scrambling of shoed feet as the hired help retreated from behind their cages and bolted for the back door.

"You know better, Linc," Belden answered.

It was a stand-off, and McLane knew it. "You better pay him, Cord," he advised softly.

Bishop's mouth dropped open. "You son-of-a-bitch!" he croaked. "You're in on this…"

"No." McLane's jaws clamped shut and he exhaled slowly through his teeth; "I just know the current market price of blooded breeding stock". He was getting pretty tired of being accused of taking sides. Damned tired. "He'll shoot you, Cord. He's killed for less." The scorn in the lawman's voice reached out to Belden, hitting its intended mark.

Trace backed away, unwinding his fingers from Bishop's tie. He shoved the man back into his chair. "Never knew you to mix into a private fight, Linc." He uncocked the pistol and balanced it in his hand before slipping it back into the holster.

"It quit being private, the day you rode into town." The marshal backed against the door, slamming it shut. Without taking his eyes off the two men, he fumbled with the lock relieved when it finally snapped shut. "It's my game now, gentlemen," the word sounded derogatory, "and you're going to play it my way." He waved the rifle at Belden's middle. "Back away from the desk, Trace." He watched as Belden did as he was told, and then swung his rifle toward Bishop. "And you put both of your hands on top of the desk, where I can see them." It took a little time for Bishop to comply, but he finally obeyed. Satisfied, the lawman continued.

"Cord didn't take any fall, Trace. You beat the hell out of him, in the whorehouse above Clancy's saloon." He swung his eyes again towards the sweating banker. "And Trace's cows didn't just happen to catch fire." He shook his head. "That was stupid, Cord. Just plain stupid." He was silent a long moment. "Pay him," he ordered.

"I will not!" Bishop exploded. His face was red, the finger-thick artery in his neck pulsing just below his ear.

Belden shrugged. "Hate like Hell for you to take another fall, Cord," he ventured. "Could be here, in the bank. Or maybe at the house," he suggested. "Man could break his neck, taking a tumble off a hill that size," Trace was staring out the window at the big white house that stood on a man-made summit just north of the town.

"There aren't going to be any more falls," McLane said flatly. He turned back to the other man. "You pay him, Cord. You don't, and his crew gets wind Charlie found a couple torches right after the fire…" He didn't finish, content to let the other man's imagination do his work.

Bishop was as stubborn as the lawman. "I'll pay him," he announced. "Right after you throw him in jail for what he did to me!" He was smirking as if he was holding all the cards in a high-stake game.

McLane laughed, and called the man's bluff. "Sure. And then we'll go to trial, Cord, and Trace can tell the whole town just where you were, and who you were with when he took his pound of flesh!"

Bishop turned varying shades of purple. His eyes flicked from McLane to Belden, finally settling on the lawman. "I'll have your job for this, McLane." He dug into his desk, fumbling for a draft. "So help me God, I'll have your job!" Shaking, he plunged his pen into the inkwell.

"Like Hell you will," McLane scoffed. "You may think you own this town, Cord, but you don't own the county." He tapped his badge. "Not yet." Reaching out, he jabbed the barrel of the rifle under the man's writing arm. "Cash, Mr. Bishop. You'll pay him for his cows in cash."

Bishop's anger swelled the skin above his collar. His fingers coiled around the pen, the pressure increasing until the point bent upward across the paper. Cursing, he flung the instrument across the room. "I'll have to get if from the drawers," he said. He waited for McLane's approval and stood up, stomping across the floor to the first teller's cage. Viciously, he jerked the drawer open, his hand hovering for a moment as he debated the wisdom of his anticipated move, a small-bore pistol just within reach of his open fingers.

"Don't even think about it, Cord," McLane had seen the man's hesitation. He watched as the banker dipped his hand into the drawer and pulled out a wad of bills.

Bishop moved to the next cashier's cage and the next, repeating the same moves. He stalked back to the desk, his hands sweating as he counted out the bills. Finished, he shoved the stack at the lawman. "I want a receipt," he fumed, trying to salvage a final bit of dignity.

McLane nodded, fingering the stack of greenbacks. Satisfied, he handed the money to Belden. "Write him out a receipt, Trace. Paid in full." He watched as Belden followed his instructions, gesturing for the man to hold the paper up. Nodding his approval, he tapped the corner of the desk with the barrel of his rifle. "Sign it, date it, and leave room for me to witness it. I want this all legal." He waited until Belden backed off, and then scrawled his signature at the very bottom of the paper. Still holding the rifle, he picked up the paper, taking great pains as he folded the sheet into neat precise quarters. "I'll hang on to this for a time," he said leveling his gaze at both men. He stuffed the document into his vest pocket, patting it into place.

"You'll rue this day, McLane," Bishop took a step toward the lawman, hesitating mid-pace when the man stopped him with a long sweeping glare. "You mark my words.."

"Shut up, Cord." McLane's voice conveyed a weariness that was more than a physical fatigue. The lawman shifted, his shoulder's squaring, then relaxing. "I've had it right up to here," he fumed, making a slicing motion across his own throat with his forefinger. "This game of cat and mouse the two of you have been playing over the years." He lifted his hand in a silent warning when both men started to object. "It's over." He forced a smile, his eyes narrowing. "This is *my* town, Cord. You don't believe me, just try something else."

There was the soft sound of laughter, Belden's mouth twitching. McLane turned his head in the man's direction. "That goes for you, too, Trace," he warned. The laughter stopped. "You've got lawyers; both of you," McLane continued. "From here on out, that's who handles your differences. Any more *accidents*, and I'll lock both of you in jail." The smile came slowly, and this time it reached almost as far as the lawman's eyes. "In the same cell," he promised. He gestured toward the door with the rifle. "You've got your money, Trace. Get out."

Belden stood his ground. "Out of the bank, Linc? Or out of town?" he asked quietly.

McLane cursed the man's stubbornness, his answer coming through clenched teeth. "For starters, out of the bank."

"I won't leave town until Doc says Lon's fit to travel," Belden said levelly. "I want you to understand that, Linc." He was quiet, his gaze shifting to Bishop. "I want Cord to understand that," he finished.

McLane's head bobbed in a single terse nod. "He understands, Trace. We both understand." He pointed toward the door a final time. "Now get out." He watched as Belden unlocked the door and departed. Satisfied, he eased the hammer back into place and canted the rifle against his right shoulder. He cast a wary eye at the still fuming Bishop. "You got off easy, Cord," he said. "In his place," he jerked his head in the direction Belden had gone, "I'd have turned my crew loose, let them collect for those cows."

"You can't prove anything!" Bishop was at the window, staring into the street, his face still beet red. "Neither one of you. Not one damned thing!!"

McLane shook his head at the man's stupidity. "You used to be a smart man, Cord," he said. "You're letting this thing with Elizabeth and the boy get in your way, muddy your thinking.

"You let your lawyer handle Trace from here on out, Cord. You don't," he faced the man, his voice quiet, "and I'm personally going to tell your wife just exactly where you were when you took that *fall*." He grinned across at the man. "Not only where, Cord; but just who was there to pick you up." Laughing, he went through the door, the sound of Bishop's cursing a sweet song on his ears.

CHAPTER 6

———

Belden was in the general store, Toby with him, rummaging through the stack of denim jeans. He picked out a pair and held them up to the kid's waist, shaking his head when he found that he had more pants than boy. Straightening, he resumed his search. The kid's waist was small; too damned small. Mrs. Cutter was with them. "You could get him suspenders, Trace. Lord only knows, he'll never fatten up, not with that trollop…" she stopped harping and shook out yet another pair of pants, measuring them with a practiced eye.

She was a good woman, Belden supposed. She had spent most of the last hour helping him outfit the boy. It was the way she talked about the kid that dug at him. Like he wasn't there; or worse, that he was somehow impaired and couldn't hear or understand what she was saying. It was as if she felt it was Toby's fault his mother was a whore; and that he was somehow to blame for her bad decisions

Finally, more in the hope the woman would leave them and her endless chatter would be over, he took the armful of clothes she had collected and shoved them in the boy's hands. "You take them back there," he pointed to the curtained back room, "try them on." He picked at the frayed collar on the boy's shirt. "And then you throw this other stuff away." The boy grinned and nodded, a peppermint stick hanging out of the corner of his mouth like a cigar.

Fletcher watched as the little boy disappeared behind the faded draperies. "You thought about how he's going to take it when we leave here?" He avoided Belden's scowl, his fingers tracing the wood grain on a piece of shelving.

Trace felt the blood rising in his neck. "I've thought about it," he growled. "I've been thinking about little else." That was true enough. In the last week, the kid had occupied a good portion of his time as well as his thoughts.

Fletcher decided to change the subject. "Saw you and Lon coming out of the Doc's office this morning. What'd he have to say about the arm?"

Same song, different tune, Belden thought. "He took the bandages off; said – considering the circumstances – everything is fine; just fine."

"Figured as much." The foreman was quiet again. He cleared his throat. "So did McLane." He shook his head when Belden started to speak. "Linc wants us out, Trace. In the morning. I told him we'd go."

Belden knotted his fingers around a flannel work shirt. "Just who the Hell do you think you are?" he seethed. He knew the question was out of line when he asked it.

Charlie shifted his weight to his good leg. "Your foreman," he answered. "The man you pay to see your ranch gets run proper, your cows get home." He stared up into Belden's face. "Tomorrow, Trace." He turned and left the man, touching the brim of his hat as he passed Mrs. Cutter.

Lon was at the counter with the woman, his back to Trace. He was nodding his head, his finger tapping at the glass on the front of the showcase. Trace watched as the

woman bent down, still angry at Fletcher; the anger growing when the woman straightened. She had a revolver in
her hand, and she gave it to the youth.

"Just what the hell do you think you're doing?" Belden
crossed the few feet to the counter.

"What's it look like?" The kid stared down at the pistol.
He rotated the cylinder, hefting the gun for balance.

Belden glanced around the store, mindful of the other
cowhands that were present. He lowered his voice. "Put it
back, Lonny," he ordered.

Lon ignored his brother, his fingers tracing the pistol's
lines. "I'll need a belt and holster," he said. "And a box
of cartridges."

Toby squeezed in between Belden and Lon, his nose
pressed into the glass. Belden passed a quick glance over
the boy and nodded his approval, reaching out to smooth
the kid's collar. He turned his gaze back to his younger
brother, his hand still on Toby's shoulder. "You aren't
buying that pistol, Lon," he said firmly.

Lon studied his brother's reflection in the smudged
glass countertop. "I got the money to pay for it, Trace."
He said the words as if they made a difference.

Belden's jaws tightened. He felt Toby tugging at his
sleeve, the boy's eyes on a bone-handled pocketknife in
the show case. Belden nodded his head, and dug into his
pocket. "The jackknife, too, Mrs. Cutter," he said. He
turned back to his brother. "I don't care if you have the
money, Lon. You're not buying a handgun." Placing some
bills and coins on the counter, he faced the woman. "You
sell him that pistol, Mrs. Cutter, I'll bring it back."

The woman took Belden's money and made change.
She handed Toby the pocketknife and then drew back her
hand. "I'm sorry, Lonny," she said softly. She waved her

upturned fingers at the youth, nodding at the revolver. "You'll have to give it back."

Lon's hand closed tighter around the weapon. Belden shook his head. He reached out, his fingers closing around Lon's write. "Put it back." He increased his grip, using his left hand to pry the boy's fingers away from the revolver's barrel.

Lon's face colored. "You've spent the last hour buyin' him anything he wants!" He pointed an accusing finger at Toby, his eyes on the pocketknife. "Me, I got my own money," he raked the younger boy with a long, bitter look. "I didn't ask you to pay for anything!"

Belden ignored the outburst. "Charlie's getting the crew ready to move out, Lon," he said patiently, aware of the faces that had been turned in their direction. "You go give him a hand." He pointed a long finger at the door.

Lon backed up a step, his fists knotted at his sides. There was a patronizing tone in Belden's voice, the same paternal disapproval that had been there ever since the incident at the stock pens. Like he was some baby who had to be reminded how to behave; a snot-nosed kid being chased away from the table for bad manners. "I'm buyin' that pistol, Trace." The resentment was in Lon's voice and his eyes. "I don't care what you say, I'm comin' back here and I will buy that pistol!"

Belden leaned against the counter, helping himself to a cigar from the glass humidor. He bit off the end, turning to face the woman, nodding in greeting as old man Cutter joined her. The words were for the older couple, as well as for his kid brother. "You buy that pistol, Lon," he said, "I'll take it away from you and bring it back here to Cutter." He swung his head toward the youth. "I'll make *you* bring it back." He watched as the boy absorbed the threat. Lon backed up a pace, shaking. He opened his mouth to say something, and then changed his mind. Back rigid, he marched across the room, kicking the screen door open. The spring howled in loud protest, recoiled, and the door slammed shut.

******

Belden took Toby for a ride; one last ride. They rode for a long time, far out into the sand hills beyond the town, both of them quiet. He hadn't said anything to the kid about leaving; couldn't say anything. And yet, he could sense that the boy knew. "Toby," he started slowing the bay to a walk.

"I want to thank you, Mr. Belden," the boy said, his eyes staring straight ahead, his head pressed against the man's right shoulder. "For the rides," he reached down, his hand stroking the bay's neck, "and for the new clothes and boots." He swallowed hard, his chest rising. "I'll never forget you, Mr. Belden," he said softly.

Trace pulled the kid closer, both arm wrapped around him. "I'll come back to see you, Toby," he promised.

"Sure, Mr. Belden," the boy replied. Others had told him the same; none of them had kept their promises.

******

McLane was waiting for them at the barn, his eyes on the boy's pinched face. He waited until Trace unloaded the kid, watching as the boy disappeared into the stable. "His mother," somehow the word didn't seem to fit, "wanted to make sure you didn't try anything funny." He reached into his vest pocket and took out a new box of snuff, cutting the lid loose with the small blade of his pocketknife. The paper peeled away like the skin of an apple; yellow, drifting to the ground. He inverted the lid and scooped out a small mound. "I don't want any trouble over Toby, Trace." The lawman worked the tobacco into his mouth, rolling it between his lower lip and gums.

Belden dismounted. "She doesn't care about that kid!" He slammed a fist into the corral gate. "Not a tinker's damn!"

McLane nodded, his jaws working. "She uses the boy. Isn't a man in town that doesn't know that." He cast a long look at Belden, the grey eyebrows almost meeting as his eyes narrowed. "Excepting you, Trace." He paused. "Cutter says you and the boys plan on buying the kid a pony before you leave; that little paint gelding." He shook his head. "Don't do it, man," the lawman advised.

Belden wasn't interested the man's advice. "The crew took a vote, and Charlie and I kicked in. What my men do with their money, what I do with *my* money, is our business; not yours." He poked the lawman in the chest with a rigid forefinger, "And sure in Hell not Cutter's."

The lawman's hand closed around Trace's wrist, and he pulled the man's finger away from his chest. "I don't give a damn what you do with your money!" He nodded toward the barn door. "You buy that kid a pony, it won't be a week until the woman has it sold and is wearing the profits on her back." He released Trace's hand, shoving it away. "Hell, she's done it before," he said it as though he knew firsthand, "and she'll do it again. I just don't see any sense buyin' the kid that kind of hurt."

"Then why don't you *fine* people," Belden jerked his thumb at the passing townsmen, his tone sarcastic, "do something?"

McLane snorted and looked at the man as if he had taken leave of his senses. "Like what, Trace?" His tone matched the other's. "The boy is hers. Lock, stock, and barrel. She could rent him out to some pig farm tomorrow, and there isn't a thing any of us can do to stop her."

Belden jammed his hands into his pockets. "I could take him, Linc," he said flatly.

McLane shifted his wad of snuff to the other side of his mouth. "You could, Trace, but you won't." He raked the man with a long, wintry stare. It was his turn to punch his finger in Belden's chest. "You hired yourself a lawyer to help you get your boy back from Bishop and the woman. How far do you think you'd get in court if they found out you'd stolen some kid that doesn't even belong to you?" The man relented, but only slightly. "Go home, Trace. Worry about your own boy, and forget Toby."

The object of their discussion emerged out of the darkness of the barn, and both men stopped talking. He saw Belden looking at him and forced a weak smile, the grin fading as he turned his gaze to McLane.

Trace waved the boy forward. "Any objections to me buying the kid supper, Linc?"

McLane shook his head, watching as the boy came towards them. "The kid's got some good times due him, Trace," he said compassionately. "No sense taking what little there is…" He spat into the dirt beside the fence, dousing a piss ant with the brown slime. Congratulating himself on his aim, he turned on his heel, and took his leave.

Belden held out his hand for the boy, his arm slipping around the youngster's sparse shoulders. "We're going to have supper with the crew, partner." He guided the boy down the street to the café, forcing a grin as he pointed through the windows to the clutch of men gathered inside. Together, they entered the restaurant, the men shouting a boisterous greeting.

Not a man had come empty handed. They gave the boy small things, things a boy could treasure. A penny whistle, a boy-sized belt and holster with a wooden gun; bags of penny candy, even a kid's slicker. Things that couldn't be bartered or sold away. Belden looked around the room, proud of the men; disappointed when he saw that Lon was not there. *Too bad*, he thought. *Let him sulk about the pistol.* Dismissing his brother from his thoughts, Belden picked up the kid, and sat the boy in the place of honor at the head of the table.

The dinner seemed to end as suddenly as it began, the men fading away like the conversation until Belden and the boy were alone. They made the long walk to the bordello, staring at their own long shadows on the boardwalk, the setting sun at their backs. Toby reached up, taking Belden's large hand in his own, saying nothing. Together, they trudged up the stairs.

The woman was in the room alone, preening in front of the mirror. Belden took off his hat, watching the woman as she studied his reflection. He could see Toby in the mirror, the boy going to the pallet in the corner, sliding down the wall, his back to the fading paper. The kid pulled his knees up to his chest and buried his head in his arms. Trace tossed his hat on the bed. He dug into his pocket and crossed to where the woman sat. A gold piece appeared between his thumb and forefinger, and he rolled it back and forth, the metal reflecting the light from the lantern. She smiled her acceptance and reached out. *It was true*, he thought grimly, reminded of their first encounter. *She'd really do it. Right here, now; with the kid watching.* He produced a second coin, sorry that he hadn't gotten Cully to bed her. "The room." He led her to the door. "I just want to rent the room."

The woman laughed. "That's what they all say," she sneered.

******

Morning came after a long sleepless night, the sun streaking the horizon a bright red. Toby lay curled against Belden's stomach, quiet, his back and shoulders growing cold. Trace silently wished he had never met the kid, and then cursed himself for knowing it wasn't true. "It's time to go, Toby," he said gently.

The boy roused. He got up without looking at Belden, taking a long time to dress. The man joined him, reaching down to refasten the kid's buttons when it became obvious the boy had done it wrong. *There were many ways a man could be selfish*, he mused. *Or a woman*. He was as guilty of using the boy as the woman was. Toby had filled a need in him, the empty void he'd felt after his confrontation with his own son; and he had used the boy to fill that emptiness without once considering what he might be doing to the child. *I am*, he chided himself, *a real first-class son-of-a-bitch*.

******

Toby followed him to Cutter's, sticking close as they thumped down the boardwalk. Trace sent him into the barn for the bay, and then headed for Cutter's house across from the stock pens.

The old man was waiting, and he responded at the first knock, waving Belden into the house. He pressed his finger against his lips. "The missus," he said. "She's still asleep." He nodded toward the closed door off the kitchen.

"We want to buy the kid that pony and the tack, Sam." Belden took a piece of paper from his pocket, along with a hundred-dollar bill. "You tell the woman you gave him a job, and in exchange, he gets to ride the pony." He scribbled out his address. "Once a month, you send me a bill for the pony's board. I'll make it good, and send a couple dollars for you to give Toby for wages.

"And, Sam," he looked across at the man. "You let me

know how he's doing."

Cutter took out a dirty handkerchief and blew his nose. He sniffled loudly. "Sure is a sorry shame that floozy ain't got her head busted by some jealous wife," he said bitterly.

Belden forced a wry grin. "Yeah," he said. The idea appealed to him more than he cared to admit. He put out his hand. Cutter pumped it like an old well.

Toby was at the door when Belden came out, his face drawn. Somehow, he had managed to saddle the bay, the horse tethered at the stock pens. Fletcher joined them, his big grey mouthing the bit, ears forward, the animal's eyes on the activity inside the pens. "We're ready, Trace," he said. He was unable to look at the kid.

Toby sucked in a lungful of air, the sound cutting into Belden like a hot knife. And then he was all over the man, his arms tight around Belden's waist. The man untangled himself and dropped to one knee, brushing the curls away from the boy's eyes. "Mr. Cutter is going to give you a job, Toby," he lied. "You're to help him out here at the stable, and if you do a good job, he'll let you ride that little paint." He held the boy by his shoulders, and felt his own chest tighten as his skin seemed to shrink. "He'll pay you, too, Toby. A dollar a week." The hair was in the kid's eyes again and Trace lifted it away. "You do right by him, Toby," the man ordered gruffly.

The kid nodded, his chin quivering. He grabbed Belden around the neck and held him, his tears warm against the man's skin. And then he was gone, pulling free, running back into the blackness beyond the stable doors. Belden started after him, only to find his way blocked by Fletcher's horse. Charlie shook his head. "Let it go, Trace. Just let it go."

Belden took the man's advice. He turned, checking the bay's cinch. He could feel the boy watching him from inside the barn, and lifted his hand to brush away a sudden chill at the back of his neck. Without looking back, he mounted, and kicked the bay into a bone-shaking trot.

Charlie came up beside him. He rolled a smoke, and then another, handing Belden the spare. "Trace," he began.

"Not now, Charlie," Belden warned. Silent, they headed out of town, pushing the cattle ahead of them, following behind the chuck wagon, the supply wagon bringing up the rear; until they were beyond the town limits and the buildings were at their backs. The men begin to fan out, forming a ragged *U* at the sides and rear of the herd; Belden and Fletcher moving forward to join the riders driving the *remuda* they had brought north from the home ranch. The farther they got from Liberty, the darker the sky, and the blacker Trace Belden's mood.

******

For two full days it rained without letting up, the herd sloughing through the mud, the pace slow, tedious. Then, on the third morning, they got a reprieve. The weather changed.

Belden did not. The harder he tried to forget the boy, the more he thought of him. He stayed in the saddle, pausing just long enough for a cup of coffee and a fresh mount. As long as he kept busy, he reasoned, he didn't have time to remember. He pulled the bay to a jolting halt, swinging down from the saddle and jerking the girth straps loose in one sweeping motion.

The saddle blanket was wet; soaked through with white sweat. He pulled it from the gelding's back, shook it out, and immediately headed for the supply wagon in search of a dry pad. He was rummaging through the sparse stack of extras when Charlie handed him a mug of coffee.

"I don't want any lectures, Charlie." Reaching out he took the mug.

"Not me, boss man." Fletcher raised his right hand Indian fashion in a sign of peace. He gestured toward the *remuda*.

Belden took a long drink of coffee, tilting his head far back as he drained the cup; welcoming the bite of the whisky Charlie had generously dosed the bitter brew. When he finished, he tipped his head back down, following the foreman's gaze. He turned slightly, handing the empty mug to Charlie, staring hard at his brother's back. "Lon," he called out, his voice frost.

Lon was busy with his sorrel. He hadn't talked to Trace since leaving Liberty, since that day in Cutter's store. "What?" he answered, still working on lacing the saddle.

Belden moved behind the youth, his right hand reaching out to touch the walnut grip of the boy's Colt. "Where'd you get it?" he asked.

"In Liberty," came the boy's sullen reply. He reached up, his hand on the saddle horn as he pulled at the rig, checking the cinch. Satisfied, he started to climb aboard, and felt Trace's hand on his shoulder.

"When?" Belden never wasted words when he was angry.

"That same day," the boy answered.

"At Cutter's?" Trace's voice was barely above a whisper. He waited for some response from the youth. There was none. "Damn it, Lon! I'm not accustomed to talking to a man's back. Turn around when I talk to you!" he demanded.

Lon's right hand balled into a fist around the saddle horn, and he rested his head against the smooth leather. He flexed his hand and turned, slowly. "I went to the sutler's store, out at the old fort." He paused, lifting his head to stare directly into his brother's eyes. "It was my money, Trace. My business."

"That's why you weren't at supper that night," Belden surmised, remembering. The anger grew. The fort was a half-day's had ride from the fort. The kid would have been gone most of the afternoon and late into the night; in territory he didn't know. "Take it off, Lon," he ordered. "Take if off and put it in the wagon." His good eye narrowed, the brow arching as the boy shook his head. "You put it in the wagon, or I'll take it away from you." There was something very ominous in Belden's voice when he said the words. When the kid still hesitated, he reached out, his left hand going to the kid's right shoulder. With his right, he began unbuckling the belt. "I catch you with this again, and there'll be Hell to pay. Pure Hell. You think on that, Lonny." He jerked the belt loose, not caring when it was obvious the sudden move had caused the youth pain. "You think on that real hard!"

Lon pulled away from the man, his face flushed. He could see the crew watching. "Give it back, Trace," he demanded, his voice rising. "Damn it! You give it back!!"

Belden shook his head. He saw Charlie approaching with a fresh mount and took the reins. "Not hardly, boy." He swung up into the saddle, reaching back to stuff the holstered pistol into his bedroll. Feeling the kiss of the north wind on his cheek, he kicked the horse into a run. There was an even greater chill at his back.

CHAPTER 7

———

The storm hit the sixth night out, one of those freak spring storms that breaks loose rolling the black clouds across the heavens like dust before an old woman's straw broom. The lightening started, booming against the ground with the earth-shaking sound of field artillery, exploding through the dark sky in bright blinding flashes that spooked cows and horses alike. For two nights not one man spread his bedroll, and the herd moved less than half a mile. It was enough just to keep them milling; contained. The men cursed; the weather, the animals, the cook, each other.

Belden tugged on Solomon's rope, snubbing the yearling at the end of the supply wagon. For two days, the animal had balked at being driven, intent on clumsy courtships aimed at heifers and mature cows alike. *He's practicing*, Fletcher observed, amused by the young bull's amorous attack on Belden's chestnut mare. Trace's humor was gone. Remembering, he jerked the calf's lead even shorter. "You try anything like that again, you little bastard, and I'll turn you to the most expensive steer in history," he promised. He tapped the animal between the eyes in farewell, and headed for the cook wagon.

Trace pulled himself up over the tailgate, his hand out for another cup of coffee and a plate of hot beans. He bent his head to blow into the mug of steaming coffee, and dumped a hatful of rain into his plate, the water spilling down from the brim of his soaked Stetson. He heaved the tin plate through the opening at the end of the wagon, and let go with all the frustration that had been locked inside for the past week, the swear words rolling up from the depth of his bowels and roaring into the storm. There was a loud clap of thunder, rumbling across the sky directly above the man's head, the wagon shaking. It was as if God had heard his blasphemies and was rebuking him, reminding the man that He, and not Belden, was in charge. As if to emphasis His point the heavens opened, torn apart by a bolt of blue-white lightening that lit up the camp like broad daylight. Belden stared out into the tempest and thought he saw a wraith-like figure plodding toward the wagon, arms outstretched like some beckoning angel. The sudden vision made Belden something more than a casual believer. There was another burst of light, this one longer, more intense than the other, and he watched awestruck as the figure came closer.

"Mr. Belden," the voice called.

It was the kid, Toby. He looked like a drowned cherub, his face white, the blond curls pasted against his head by the rain, his yellow slicker iridescent in the lightening. Belden jumped out of the wagon and reached out to him, pulling him close, his heart pumping. The rain poured down on them, and he could feel the kid shivering. He hoisted the child into the wagon and climbed in behind him.

The boy was soaked through, his head bare, a thin vapor rising from the small body. The cook stared across at him, and then poured a big mug of coffee, dosing it liberally with canned milk, sugar and a generous splash of medicinal rye.

"For Christ's sake," he said, shaking his head. He pressed the cup into the boy's hands, repeating the words. Then, recovering, he began issuing orders. "Get him out of those wet clothes, Trace." The old man was a flurry of movement, his arms digging into the old chest behind his seat. He pulled out a woolen blanket, draping it around the boy's naked shoulders, watching like a mother hen as Belden removed the kid's boots. They were full of water, cold water, and when Trace removed his socks, the boy's feet were blue.

They stripped him naked, Belden rubbing him down with double layers of cotton flour sacking. Pictures began forming in the man's mind, images of all the things that could have happened to the boy, wandering alone in the storm. "Why, Toby?" his words gruffer than he intended. He was drying the boy's hair, rubbing hard.

"She found out about the pony, Mr. Belden." The boy's voice was muffled by the sacking, and the man stopped rubbing, not sure of what he had heard.

"What?" he asked, pulling the rag away from the boy's face.

"She found out about the pony," the boy repeated. He stared up at Belden, the pale eyes filling. "Mr. Cutter. He got drunk, and Mama..." the boy couldn't finish. "She sold him, Mr. Belden. She sold my horse." He swallowed hard, water streaming down his cheeks.

The kid was crying, trying hard not to, his eyes blinking rapidly. Belden handed him the sack. "Wipe that rain off your face, Toby. You're dripping all over the floor." Squatting back on his heels, Belden thought of the woman, sorry that he hadn't strangled her that first night. He nodded at the cup of doctored coffee the boy still clutched in his hands. "You drink that. All of it." The kid made a face but did as he was told, Belden watching him closely. He turned to the cook. "Keep an eye on him, Eli."

The old man scratched his beard and grinned, display-ing a mouthful of gums. "I'll watch him, Trace. I'll watch him real good," he promised. He fished into the trunk and pulled out a small cushion; the one he reserved for his aching bones when the long hours in the driver's seat left him stiff-legged and barely able to move. Tucking the boy in, he waved Belden off into the night.

******

Belden returned to the wagon at dawn, pausing to enjoy the clear sky, the sun bright yellow on a cloudless hori-zon. Charlie and Lon were with him, trailing behind as he led the way to the wagon. He dismounted and held back the canvas flap, motioning his two companions forward. Charlie stared down at the still sleeping boy. "What the Hell," he breathed softly.

"He came in last night," Belden said. "He walked, Charlie. I don't know how he did it, but he walked."

Charlie's face softened, a look of awe spreading across his lined forehead. "Well, I'll be …," he whispered, reach-ing out to touch the kid's head. He turned to face Belden. "The paint?" he asked.

Belden gritted his teeth, lowering his voice when he saw Toby stir beneath the grey blanket. "The woman got wise to what we did. She got Cutter drunk and the old fool told her. She sold it."

Fletcher considered the man's words. "What are you going to do, Trace?"

"Take him back," Lon's voice answered before Belden could reply. The youth's face was white, his lips a tight line.

"No." Belden shook his head. He stood for a time, silent, studying his brother's face. There was something in Lon's eyes; the same growing defiance he had seen the morning he had taken the pistol away from the boy.

"McLane will come after him," Lon argued. "You know what he said about the kid…"

"Then he'll come," Belden said quietly. He lifted his hand when Lon started to object. "I can't spare the time, Lon. We've come too far, and we're still a week behind of where we should be. I can't spare the time, or the men."

Lon was adamant. "*I'll* take him back," he said stubbornly. He reached into the wagon, intending to shake the boy awake.

Belden probed the child's face again, his fingers closing around Lon's outstretched arm. There was more there than concern about McLane. "We're taking him with us, Lonny," he said; his tone suggesting that he would tolerate no more arguments.

Lon was thinking it over. His eyes locked onto the sleeping boy. *It was going to be Liberty all over again, the same thing. Trace all wrapped up in the little bastard, the kid tagging along after him. Everywhere.* He started to say something, his eyes meeting Trace's only briefly, then changed his mind. He retreated across the campsite to disappear among the horses in the *remuda*.

Belden turned to face his foreman, expecting more trouble. "You have anything you want to say, Charlie?" he asked softly.

"You think he's warm enough?" Fletcher reached into the wagon and pulled the blanket up around the kid's shoulders.

******

The crew made a joke out of it, how the sunshine seemed to have followed the kid into camp. It didn't even seem to matter anymore that they were still up to their rear ends in mud. What mattered was that the kid was there; that he was with them. Even Lon seemed to relent, his resentment over the boy's presence seeming to mellow as soon as Trace made it clear he would be contacting McLane once they reached Laredo.

Toby wasn't concerned one way or the other. He was too busy with the here and now. He had learned to laugh again, the kind of spontaneous laughter that rolled up from deep inside, without waiting anymore for the approval of the others. He would throw back his head, the blond curls dancing around his face, his hands pressed against his belly, and the laughter would just come. Infectious, over anything.

There was another change in the camp, one that put the entire crew in the kid's everlasting debt. Eli, the cook, was seriously plying his chosen trade again. He was cooking, really cooking, and for that miracle, not one man in camp would have hesitated to mortgage his soul on the boy's behalf. Trace made the mistake of commenting on the old man's recent culinary feats and had his ears blistered, the cook dumping his piece of dried apple pie into the middle of his stewed beef. *A growing boy needs to eat, you ignorant bastard!!* The old man fumed. Belden retreated from the cook wagon a humble and educated man.

Ten days out, Belden and Charlie spotted a lone wagon silhouetted against the stark horizon, the right rear wheel pulled. A lean figure in a linen shirt struggled with a crude lever, patiently laboring to make the repairs. The two men pulled their mounts to a halt, staying well out of fire range. They watched as the man continued his labors. Charlie spoke first, handing Trace the army issue telescope from his saddlebags. "What do you think, Trace?"

Belden adjusted the glass, sweeping the area around the wagon. "Sodbuster," he grimaced, snapping the glass shut against his palm.

Charlie took the scope and made his own investigation, pausing to eye the lone figure seated on a blanket in the grass beside the wagon. "He's got a woman with him," he said. He shifted in the saddle, massaging the stiffness in his game leg.

"And just what am I supposed to do about that?" Belden screwed around in his saddle and faced his foreman, staring into the man's impassive face.

"Hell, Trace, I wouldn't have nary a thought about that," the man paused to cut himself a plug of tobacco. "Me just being the straw boss of this here outfit, pushing the little cows here and there. Just a crippled old vet'ran, tryin' to hold on to his job..."

"Oh, Sweet Jesus," Belden moaned. He raised both hands in a gesture of total submission, hoping to silence the man. Nudging the bay in the sides, he pushed by Fletcher. "Well, what are you waiting for?" he called over his shoulder. Charlie grinned at the man's back and together they headed for the farmer's wagon.

The farmer backed up at the sound of shod horses, his hand disappearing inside the wagon, reappearing with a Spencer carbine. He cradled the piece in his arms, wary. "Mornin'," he greeted, shading his eyes as he looked behind the two riders.

Trace returned the salute, and kept both hands locked on top of his saddle horn. The farmer's rifle was well cared for, clean. "The name's Belden. This is my foremen, Charlie Fletcher. We've got a small bunch of cattle, about two miles back," he said. "We're on our way home." He scanned the man's campsite again, rising slightly in his stirrups when he saw a coffee-brown mare tethered behind the wagon. She was small, compact. Just the right size for a kid.

The farmer read the look and chose to ignore it. "Name's Lassiter. Frank Lassiter." He nodded at the woman, his face drawn. "My wife…" he cleared his throat, and his face clouded, aging him.

Belden's eyes were still on the mare. "Your family in the wagon?"

Lassiter shook his head, his voice lowering. "My family is dead," he declared, his eyes on the woman again.

Unbidden, Charlie dismounted. "We'll give you a hand, mister," he said. Hesitantly, Belden climbed down beside him, leading the horses to the off side of the wagon. He knotted the reins in the iron hitch ring.

They had to partially unload the wagon, aware of the woman's empty eyes on them as they carefully stacked her belongings in the grass. Charlie bellied his way underneath the prairie schooner, cursing as he surveyed the damage, his shirt stained grass-green as he slid back out. Standing up, he brushed himself off. "You got more than a bad wheel, Lassiter." He stared off into the treeless plain. "The axel is split. Not clear through, but enough that she'll snap first good bounce." He faced the man. "I didn't see no spare," he said.

The man squared his thin shoulders, and behind him the woman let out a long, anguished sob. "Back there," Lassiter jerked his head in the direction from which they had come. "At the river. We snapped the front axle when we made the crossing." He dragged a weary arm across his eyes, his shoulders sagging under some unseen weight.

"Don't rain, that it don't pour," Charlie breathed. He tugged at Belden's sleeve, and the two exchanged a long look, Trace finally nodding his head. Without speaking, Charlie mounted his horse and headed back toward the herd.

Fletcher returned with the supply wagon, scrambling underneath to unlash the spare axle. The gentle lowing of the cows came to them from behind a grassy knoll, the cook wagon appearing over the ridge. Toby jumped down from the wagon, fell, and then righted himself. He trotted over, eager to help.

The kid was everywhere, poking his nose into the pile of furnishings, edging closer to the brown pony, his mouth going as fast as his feet. "Did you see him, Mr. Belden?" He ran up to where Trace was working on the wheel, poking his head in front of the man as he checked his progress. "Didja see him?" he asked again.

"Her," Belden corrected, lifting the kid out of the way.

"Ain't she a beaut?" the kid breathed. He spotted the woman and was off again before Belden could grab him. The man cursed and stood up, wiping his hand in the long grass, his fingers slick with axle grease.

He trod the few paces to where the woman sat, feeling the intruder, bothered by the vacant eyes. "Ma'am," he greeted.

Toby was hunkered down in front of her, his eyes on her large belly. "She's going to have a baby," he said with an air of authority, reaching out to touch her.

Oh, Jesus. Belden could feel the redness creeping up his neck. Reaching out, he looped an arm around the kid's waist and swept him up off the blanket. He couldn't get away fast enough. "Boy, you're going to make an old man out of me long before my time." He sat the boy down on the ground, his hand firmly planted on the kid's shoulder. "Toby," he began. "You don't go where you haven't been invited," he scolded. "That lady," he continued, "is sick. She doesn't need you poking around, asking questions."

Toby worked the thing over in his mind. "Okay, Trace," he said. And that was it.

The old cook did himself proud again at supper. The smell of dried apples, raisins and brown sugar drifted on the night air, blending with the rich aroma of coffee, salt pork and biscuits. He heaped a plate high and handed it to Toby, watching as the kid carefully carried it to where the woman sat.

Belden was at the fire, the farmer joining him. "I see you have some hurt animals, Mr. Belden." Lassiter sprawled his lanky frame beside the fire, his eyes on the flames. "I'm a fair hand with that kind of doctoring," he offered.

"Then I'd appreciate you taking a look at my cows, Mr. Lassiter; soon as we finish supper." Belden understood a man's need to repay a favor.

Lassiter had underestimated his talents. Sleeves rolled up, he spent the rest of the evening working his way through the herd, his fingers probing and digging at the cattle with a sureness that seemed inborn. He signaled for more light, dropping to his knees beside a downed cow. Her calf was beside her, rooting in the grass for the unexposed teats. Belden lowered the lantern he was carrying, watching as Lassiter examined the cow and tried unsuccessfully to coax her to her feet. "Bad strain," he said. "Here," he smoothed his flat palm across the Hereford's right shoulder and down her foreleg. He took Belden's free hand and pressed it against the cow's side. Trace could feel the heat. "There isn't any fracture, Mr. Belden, but she's hurt."

Trace helped the man to his feet. "We were in mud, had a bunch of cows mired pretty deep." He stared down at the cow. The animal had been falling behind with each passing day; enough that she had become a source of aggravation. "Must have hurt her when we pulled her out."

Lassiter nodded. "With proper rest, some liniment, she'll come around." He shook his head. "Be a shame to lose a fine animal like that, just for the lack of a few days' rest."

Belden had never thought of it before, a dirt farmer appreciating the value of a good beef cow. Farmers meant fences, and fences meant no free range. He cleared his throat, thinking of the little mare. "I'd like to make a trade, Lassiter." He lifted the globe on the lantern, lighting a smoke and handing it to the other before lighting his own. "One lame cow with calf, for one pony. With some cash thrown in if you have tack."

"For your boy," he reasoned. The man inhaled, clearly enjoying the smoke. He took another puff, then pinched the cigarette out before carefully putting it into his shirt pocket. He faced Belden, his skin pale in the dim light of the lantern. "That's why you decided to help us." There was no malice, no accusation in the man's voice. "Because of the pony."

Belden nodded his head. "I'm not as inclined as my foreman to perform acts of Christian kindness, Mr. Lassiter." He took a long drag on the cigarette. "I'm a good hundred miles short of where I planned to be with the herd, and I want to go home.

"I would never have crawled under that wagon," he said. "I would have just helped with the wheel, just enough to soothe my conscience. And then I would have ridden off without ever looking back."

Lassiter shook his head slowly. He had seen Belden with the boy and the animals. "I don't believe that, Mr. Belden." He kicked at a dry pile of cow chips. "I'll have to talk to my wife. The pony belonged to our boy…" his voice drifted off like the smoke from Belden's cigarette. He coughed, staring into the darkness. "We'll need a cow, what with the child coming soon," he said. He was aware a Hereford wouldn't be the most bountiful source of milk, but she had a suckling calf; and some was better than nothing at all.

Belden watched as the man walked off into the blackness at the edge of the campfire. He knew that pony or no pony, he would leave the man the cow and the calf.

******

They rolled out at the first light of dawn, a grey mist billowing above the ground that reached up to the Herefords' bellies and made the animals appear legless above the fog. It took Belden and two other to get the injured cow on her feet. He led her to the rear of Lassiter's wagon and tied her off, mindful of the noise when the calf began to suckle. The farmer and his wife were still asleep, the canvas flap still tied shut. Resolutely, Belden started back toward the cook wagon, cutting through the morning mist, in need of his cup of coffee. Charlie greeted him, a tin mug in his outstretched hand. Lon was sulking beside the wagon, his eyes on the Hereford. "We could have butchered her for meat, Trace," he groused.

"We could have. I chose not to." Belden was in no mood to be questioned about his decision. He downed the coffee and held out his cup for a refill.

"Mr. Belden?"

It came as a shock, the gentle sound of a woman's voice out there in the middle of nowhere. The three turned, sweeping their hats from their heads, facing the woman. She was alone, a knitted shawl around her shoulders, a paper wrapped bundle in her arms. "Frank told me about the boy, about you wanting the pony for him." She hesitated. "We want you to have the pony." She turned slightly, nodding toward the wagon. Lassiter was saddling the mare. When the woman faced Belden again, there was a quiet calm in her, the stricken look of the day before less intense. She placed a hand on her stomach. "I have to think of this child now." She stretched out her arms, again offering the bundle she had been holding. "There are some clothes in here. Shirts, pants…" Without finishing, she turned and walked quickly away.

"Toby." Belden called softly to the boy, still watching after the woman. The youngster dropped to the ground beside him, and he could see from the kid's face that he had been listening. He showed him the bundle of clothing and then placed it in the wagon. "I want you to thank them, Toby. For the clothes and the pony. And you give this," he pressed a Bull Durham sack into the boy's hand, "to Mr. Lassiter."

The kid nodded his head and took off at a run, catching up with the woman. He reached out, taking her hand, walking with her to where Lassiter stood waiting. They visited for a time, and then Lassiter lifted his hand in farewell. He picked up the boy and sat him on the pony, handing him the reins. The kid looked ten feet tall.

Fletcher was beside Belden. He'd seen the Bull Durham sack when Trace handed it to the boy; and watched as Toby delivered it to the sodbuster. "How much?" he asked.

"What I had left of my tobacco and some papers," he smiled, thinking of how surprised the farmer would be when he rolled his first smoke, "the cow, the calf and fifty dollars." He was rewarded with an approving slap on the back.

The boy rode with Belden that morning. He kept plow-reining the mare, and Trace reached across, threading the lines until the boy held both in one hand, one strap under his thumb, the other between his ring and little finger. "I don't want you riding her on your own, Toby." Leaning out of his saddle, he reached down to pull the boy's leg back until the ball of his foot rested in the cradle of the stirrup. "You ride with me or Charlie. But not alone."

The boy nodded his head and adjusted his other leg so that foot was the same as the other. "Her name's Lady," he said. He turned, facing Belden. "Mrs. Lassiter kissed me," his blue eyes were big. "When I told her *thank you*, she kissed me." He touched his cheek.

That, Belden thought, remembering the kid's mother, *was probably a first.*

CHAPTER 8

The days passed with a long, weary sameness. The muck and mud that had plagued the cattlemen became dust, dust that seemed to permeate everything, no matter how tight the seal, or close the weave. It was in the food they ate, in the clothes they wore; matted on the eyelashes of both man and animal alike. Only Toby seemed unaffected by the dirt. He was thriving, his once thin cheeks filled out, laugh lines creasing the skin under his eyes. Even now, riding drag with Trace and Lon, the boy's eyes seemed to dance above the faded blue kerchief covering his nose and mouth. He reached up and lifted the mask away from his chin, blowing the dust before him. "When you going to teach me to rope, Trace?" he asked, fingering the old rope Lon had given him. He started to cough.

Belden reached out and pulled the kid's bandanna back across his mouth. "You keep that thing on, Toby," he mumbled through his own. He saw the boy's shoulders droop at his reprimand, and relented. "Later," he promised, and received a mouthful of fine grit as a reward. "Just don't try anything on your own."

The cattle began bellowing, the leaders relaying a message that passed back through the herd, the noise growing in volume. "Water." Lon pointed to a line of trees poking above the hills. He kicked his gelding into a trot as the herd picked up its pace.

The cows began to fan out, the point riders weaving in and out among the moving cattle, forcing the Herefords apart as the outriders opened up their halves of the U and allowed the cows to drift. They topped a small rise and then went down a gradual incline, moving the cattle ahead of them, stringing the animals out in a long line as the approached the bank.

Fletcher pulled up beside Trace, the cook wagon close behind him. "Eli says we're going to need water, Trace." He nodded towards the wooden barrels that were strapped to the wagon's sides.

Belden pried the scarf away from his face, taking a deep breath as the dust finally settled. "We'll set up camp here, give them a rest." He stared out at the river. "We aren't going to be able to make the ford here, Charlie. Not this trip." The water was up, well into the tree line.

Lon was at the water's edge, standing beside his horse, his eyes on the far bank. He stooped over, scooping up some water in his hand, splashing it on his face and neck. Toby was on foot, too, watching. Lon bent over again, this time using his hat as a scoop, his rear end exposed. Belden watched as Toby took aim and charged.

The boy's sense of direction was fine, just fine. He placed his outstretched palms squarely on Lon's hip pockets and shoved, sliding to a halt at the river's edge. Lon was dumped headfirst into the water. He thrashed around, arms flailing wildly, his horse bolting and racing away from the water. A cow stepped daintily into the shallows, paused, and then

stretched out her neck, curious. Lon surfaced, face to face
with the interested Hereford. She stuck out her long tongue
and swiped it across his mouth. Toby fell over, rolling on
the ground, doubled up and shrieking with laughter. The
crew joined in. Lon stood up and swatted at the cow with his
water-soaked J.B., his face contorted with a look of white
rage. Belden kicked his horse in the sides and trotted toward
the river, hazing Lon's mount back to the embankment.

Lon was making his way back to shore, sloshing waist deep
in the water, and he reached Toby before Belden. He picked
the kid up, one hand on the boy's ankle, the other tangled in his
long hair. With one might heave, he sent the kid flying.

Belden was on the bank, one foot thrown over the pommel of his saddle. He rolled a smoke, spitting the pieces
of flaked tobacco as he lit up. "Lose your sense of humor,
Lon?" he asked innocently, fighting the laughter.

Lon flashed his elder brother a hot look. "Go to Hell!"
He wiped the mud from his chin with his wet sleeve, "and
you can take that kid and shove him up your ...." He
stopped mid-sentence.

"Fish him out, Lon," Belden ordered.

Lon waded back into the stream. Maliciously, he
grabbed Toby by the hair and shoved his head under the
water. He held him, briefly, as if struggling to get a better
hold. Finally, he pulled the kid out, his fingers still tightly
entwined in the boy's shaggy mane. Aware that Trace was
still behind him, watching him, he kept his voice low. "You
pull anything like that again and I'll kick your butt all the
way back to Liberty." He let go, giving the boy a shove and
pushing him towards the shore. Jaws tight, he stalked back
to the bank, his eyes straight ahead as he passed his brother.

Belden guided the bay into the river and reached out a
hand to the little boy. He pulled the kid out of the water

and hauled him back to the shore, depositing him on the grass at the water's edge.

Toby was sniffling, his eyes wide. "I can't swim," he whispered, shaking. "He hurt me, too," he whined, rubbing his head, a clump of hair missing where Lon had grabbed him.

Belden was unsympathetic. He dismounted. "You play with the big boys, you better learn to take your lumps and keep your mouth shut." He pointed the kid in the direction of the wagons. "You get yourself into some dry clothes, find Lon, and tell him you're sorry."

"It was a joke! A practical joke!!" The kid stamped his foot, objecting loudly, his chin thrust out petulantly.

"There isn't such a thing as a *practical* joke, Toby," Belden admonished. He put his fingers on the boy's mouth when the kid started to object. "Do you know what the word practical means?" He didn't wait or an answer. "It means something useful, sensible." He was running out of words he thought the boy would understand. "There wasn't anything useful or sensible about shoving Lon into the river." Finished with his lecture, he pointed at the wagon. "Solomon needs water, Toby, and I want him staked out where he can get to some grass." Putting his hands on the kid's shoulders, he turned him around and pushed him in the appropriate direction, helping him along with a solid swat to his damp rear end. Subdued, the kid trotted off.

The respite was brief. Toby attended to the bull calf, and then embarked on a series of misadventures, democratic in his choice of victims. It was as if his sojourn in the water had been a kind of rebirth. He had suddenly discovered all the natural hell-raising instincts of the very young, and nothing was sacred.

"Don't suppose he's still young enough to need a nap?" Charlie struggled with a water barrel, lashing it back in place on the side of the wagon, his tone hopeful as he spoke to Trace. Cautiously, he toed the barrel's lid from where it lay beside the wagon and flipped it over. Toby had hidden a snake under the other one, and the foreman wasn't taking any chances.

"Young enough," Belden answered, "just not willing." He picked up the lid, dusting it off before placing it on top of the barrel. Holding it even, he tamped in place with his fist."

"Oh, Lord," Charlie breathed. He blanched, the ruddy coloring in his face fading. He pointed over Trace's shoulder, speechless.

Belden turned and felt himself age ten years. He vaulted into his saddle and kicked the bay into a run, bellowing for his brother. "Lon!!"

Toby was on foot, his rope tangled around a calf, his back to the nervous mother. She stood behind him, rocking back and forth on her forelegs, her massive head swaying, eyes big. She was making quick little snorting sounds, her nostrils flaring with each breath. The other cows began to back away, opening the narrow path that led to the unknowing child. Lon spurred his horse into a run, cutting between the cow and Toby, his rope whistling as it whipped through the air. Belden tore past Lon at a gallop and reached down, grabbing the kid's belt and jerking him up from the ground.

"Goddammit, Trace!" Toby yelled. "What the Hell did you go and do that for?!"

Belden held the boy suspended above the ground, his arm outstretched, and the muscles standing out in his bunched shoulders as he slowly rotated the kid until he faced the calf's mama. Lon let up on the slack and gave the kid a good look. Nose to nose.

Counting silently to ten first in Spanish and then in English, Belden lowered the struggling boy to the ground. "… ten," he said aloud, the cords in his neck standing out. He shook a finger at the ungrateful recipient of his rescue efforts. "You get that rope off that calf," he ordered. "And then you get your butt over to the cook wagon!" The boy straightened, a belligerent pout on his face. He stood his ground until Belden urged his mount a step forward in his direction, and then he turned. Stiff-backed, Toby marched over to the calf. He pulled the noose from around the animal's neck, and then stood there, his back to the man, taking his own sweet time as he coiled the rope. Finally done, he turned and headed for the wagon. Trace followed him, leaning down from his saddle to pick up the reins of the kid's pony.

Belden dismounted, ground-hitching the bay. He ignored the kid's accusatory stare, deliberately slow as he picketed the little mare. Without speaking, he unlaced the pony's saddle and pulled it free. The kid watched every move, his lips a tight line, their eyes meeting when Trace dumped the saddle into the rear of the wagon. The man spread the sweat-soaked blanket on top of the rig, smoothing it in place. He folded his arms across the damp wool. "Toby," he began. "I told you before. You don't ride that pony, you don't try working the cows, unless one of us are with you." He tapped the kid's chest with a rigid finger, a poke for each word. "I meant it." The boy's chin thrust out stubbornly as Belden continued. "And I don't want to hear you ever swear like that again."

"You swear!" the accused said defiantly. "And so does Lon!"

Belden nodded his head. "That's right," he said, ignoring the reference to Lon. "I also drink whiskey, play cards, and smoke cigars." He left out the part about chasing women. "All things you can do, soon as you're full grown!" He finished his speech, his index finger still o the boy's chest. "You stay in the wagon, out of trouble," he instructed.

He turned from the boy and went back to the gelding and started to climb aboard.

"How long?" Toby demanded loudly.

Belden inhaled and felt the hair at the nape of his neck bristle. He eased back down onto the ground, both hands still on the saddle. "For the rest of the day, Toby," he answered.

"I ain't staying in this damn wagon," the boy answered back.

Belden swung up into the saddle and moved the bay close to the tailgate, glaring down at the kid. "You're staying in this wagon," he repeated. "You don't, I'll paddle you're a..." he stopped, "...rear end," he finished. He pulled the bay's head around, and found himself face to face with his younger brother.

Lon grinned up at the man. "Lose your sense of humor, big brother?" he asked sarcastically.

"Don't push it, Lonny. You're not that far away from buying a piece of what he's about to collect." Belden shoved by the youth, calling for Fletcher.

Charlie came up beside Belden. He'd been close enough that he'd heard the exchanges between Trace, Toby and Lon. Secretly, he hoped that Belden had finally had his fill. Not wanting to trespass and eager to appease the man's bad temper, he offered Belden his tobacco and papers. "Where you figure on crossin' this thing?" He gestured toward the river with a careless wave of his arm.

Trace shook his head, pulling his last store bought from his shirt pocket. He crimped the smoke back into its original shape. "Don't know yet," he said, eyeing the swollen river. "I've only seen it this high once before, and that was years ago." The two men threaded their way through the line of cows at the water's edge. "We'll just have to scout along the bank. South, I think; see what we have to deal with."

"What about Lander's Crossing?" The foreman was having trouble getting his cigarette lit, the tobacco sweat damp, and he bummed Belden's smoke for a start.

"I don't think so," Trace said, taking the cigarette back, "dealing with that old mule skinner is like trying to bargain with the Wootens. He'll take one look at the Herefords, and charge me bounty. And a cow for every ten we push across!"

Charlie pulled his horse to a stop, his eyes on the far hills on the other side of the river. "Well, one thing's certain. We got to cross her. She's all that stands between us and home." He nudged the grey in the flanks and followed after Belden as they began to ride single file along the shore.

They rode south, following the winding river. The further they rode, the worse it looked, the river spilling over its bank and in some places widening into a near lake. Disheartened, Belden reined in, shading his eye as he stared up at the sun. "We'll head in for noon meal," he said, turning the bay's nose back toward camp. "North," he reckoned. "We'll try following her north later this afternoon.

******

Toby pouted all through the noon meal, glowering at Belden from his perch in the wagon, his hat pulled down low on his forehead, his eyes hidden. Charlie shook a fork in the boy's direction. "The longer he hangs around you, Trace, the more he gets to actin' just like you!" He dug into his plate, still watching the kid.

Belden looked over his shoulder at Toby and quickly turned away. The boy was leaning back against the wall of the wagon, propped up on a sack of flour, his arms folded across his chest. His untouched plate sat at his side. Belden shrugged, not entirely displeased with Charlie's observation. "Stubborn little blister," he noted.

"That's what I just said. You, Lon and Toby." He took another bite of side meat. "Three peas in a pod." Before Belden
could respond, he leaned forward, his tone secretive. "Five will
get you ten he leaves that wagon next time you turn your back."

Belden glanced at the kid again, feeling smug. "He
stayed put while we were riding the bank." He considered
the wager and stuck out his hand. "I'll take that bet, Charlie." His brow knotted as he reconsidered, and he withdrew
his hand. "You ride with me when I head upriver," he said.

Charlie cast a benign look at his employer, a bucolic
look on his face. "Why, Trace! You sound like you think
I'd try and talk the kid into something." He looked hurt.

Belden nodded his head, remembering a lifetime of
wagers with the man. "You're damned right you would,"
he replied. He watched the man's eyes, saw the sparkle
dim somewhat, and allowed him to finally take his hand.

"I'll ride with you, but make it ten to twenty." Fletcher
shook Belden's hand.

Belden stood up and took his plate back to the wagon.
"Good food, old man," he said, addressing the cook. He
reached out and fingered the boy's full plate. The kid pretended he wasn't there. "Charlie and I are going to scout
the river north of here," Belden was still talking to the
cook. "See if we can't find something this side of old man
Lander's where we can make the ford."

The cook nodded, taking Belden's plate and scraping
the scraps into a slop bucket at his feet. "You goin' to make
it back for supper?"

Belden shrugged. "I don't know. We've got about
twelve miles to ride before we hit the Crossing. If we don't
find anything, I'll have to spend some time dickering with
the old bastard."

Toby snorted and reached up a hand to pull his hat farther down on his forehead. He silently mouthed Belden's curse. The man ignored him, gave his own hat a tug, and headed for the picket line and a fresh mount.

CHAPTER 9

——

Lon watched as Trace and Charlie Fletcher pointed their horses north along the river. He waited until they were out of sight and then took his own plate back to the cook wagon; his gait increasing as he spotted Cully. "Hey, Cully?"

The puncher turned and gave a small wave. "What's up, Lonny?" At twenty-two, Cully had the look of a man used to privation. He had ridden for Belden since he was twelve, and despite his youth was Fletcher's undisputed *segundo*.

"I need a favor, Cully." Lon handed his plate to the cook.

"It'll cost," Cully answered. He scraped his own plate and tossed it into the pan of soapy water on the tailgate.

Lon nodded his head. Everything that Cully did outside of his regular job had a price. "I want you to ride my spot this afternoon."

Cully took out his pocketknife and pared off a piece of chewing tobacco from the chunk he stored in an old snuff tin. "Two dollars," he said, shoving the chunk into his mouth.

"That's fifty cents an hour," Lon ciphered. "Two days wages!" He shook his head. "A dollar," he bartered.

Cully shook his head in refusal. "This is the second time in three days, Lonny. I gave you a break the last time. We keep doin' this, it'll cost me a more for liniment than what you're payin'." He grinned across at the youth.

"Charlie said they hung your old man for bein' a horse thief!" Lon took an edge off the words with a wide grin. "He couldn't hold a candle to you; not on his best day." The smile grew. "A dollar and a half," he ventured. That's what he had paid the last time.

"Uh-uh," Cully answered, his brown eyes chestnut hard. "Wouldn't want my old man turnin' over in his grave thinkin' I couldn't carry on a fine family tradition." He held out his hand. "Two dollars or you ride your own spot." Cully knew that Lon had already asked others, and had been turned down.

Reluctantly, Lon dug into his pocket. "You don't tell Trace," he said, pulling out two silver coins.

"It costs extra for a lie," Cully warned. The brown eyes warmed a little. "He doesn't ask, I won't volunteer." He shoved the money into his front pocket and headed for the picket line.

Lon was still at the cook wagon. He climbed up over the tailgate, and began rummaging in this brother's gear; working his way to where Toby sat huddled on the sack of flour.

"What'cha lookin' for?" Toby shoved his hat back, moving his legs as Lon probed deeper into the litter on the wagon floor.

"My pistol," the youth answered. "You seen it?"

Toby nodded his head. "Yeah." He turned and dug behind the flour sack. "Trace said you couldn't have it," he said.

"So?"

Toby's fingers closed around the leather belt. He hesitated. "So you'll get in trouble if he finds out," he reasoned. He hoisted the belt and holster out from its hiding place.

"He isn't going to find out." Lon took the belt and eased it into place around his slim waist.

Toby leaned against the side of the wagon, his chin resting on his arms as he stared into Lon's face. "I could tell," he said, his head cocked.

Lon's fingers slowed. He chewed at his bottom lip, his eyes on his belt buckle. "You want to come along?" he asked quietly. He lifted his head, a smile pulling at the corner of his mouth. "Trace is going to gone all afternoon, Toby. We could go for a ride," he cajoled, his eyes on the boy's face. "I'll let you shoot the pistol."

Toby's head came up off his arms. He swung his eyes toward the cook. "He'll tell," he said.

"Ain't none of his business," Lon grinned. "Is it, old man?"

"That's right, Lonny. Ain't none of my business." Eli cast a long look at both boys. "You know what Trace told you; both of you. If you ain't got enough sense to listen…" The old man went back to his dishes.

Toby stood up. "Will you teach me how to rope?" he asked.

"You going to keep your mouth shut?" Lon returned, still bargaining.

"Yeah, Lon. I won't say nothin'." Toby scrambled over the side of the wagon. He trotted alongside Lon as they headed to where their horses were tethered. "What're you gonna shoot, Lonny?" It was the first of a long line of questions.

******

Belton and Fletcher rode at a gentle lope, staying close to the river's edge. For over five miles it was the same as it had been to the south, the river flooding up and over the old shoreline. The water was high, and the current swift.

"Trace," Fletcher stretched out an arm and pulled his

horse to an abrupt stop.

Belden followed the man's pointing finger and saw what had been a stand of young trees and saplings, the stumps pointing into the air like skinned fingers. A double row of stakes led into the water, separated by a well-trodden path, wide at the opening, narrowing as it led to the water's edge. "I'll be damned," he said. "A causeway! An honest to God causeway!" He clucked to his horse, Charlie beside him.

They stared into the water, still not believing. About six inches beneath the surface of the flowing water lay an earthen bridgework, stretching out into the river. Belden dismounted and examined the row of stakes at his left, his fingernails biting into a peeled log. Charlie was on his right, checking the windrow on that side. "It hasn't been here very long, not from the look of the scars on this timber." Trace lifted a hand to his forehead, shading his good eye against the reflection of the sun on the surface of the water, searching the opposite bank for the other end of the causeway. He could hear Fletcher behind him, the steady *thwack* of the man's hand ax beating a cadence against the trunk of a young sapling. The foreman kicked the small tree over with his foot, and methodically began chopping again, trimming away the branches. Belden turned back to the water, watching as an uprooted tree drifted toward the submerged passageway. The cottonwood butted into the causeway, hung up for a brief time, and then sailed on, its journey uninterrupted.

"I got the feeling we better walk her with a pole," Charlie said, dragging the sapling toward the entrance to the passageway.

"I got a feeling you're right." Belden pointed to the floating cottonwood.

They spent a long hour crossing the causeway, probing ahead of them with the pole. There were two large holes where the packed dirt and deadwood had eroded away, and they marked, them. Charlie mopped a damp arm across his forehead, his face green. "What you think, Trace?"

Belden was thinking, his hands thumbs hooked into his waist band, his fingers slapping his pockets. "A day, maybe two. We can put half the crew to work on the causeway, while the rest of them bring the cattle up the bank." He grinned into his foreman's pale face. "That's if nobody else gets seasick."

"Kiss my arse!" Fletcher's color was slowly returning to its natural ruddiness, and they started back across the water, wading shin deep. The foreman stared straight ahead, his hand caressing his stomach. "Sure would never do for me to have to go to sea." He shook his head carefully. "I watch that water move, and the next thing I know my gut is up in my throat having a conversation with my tongue!"

Belden reached out and clapped the man between the shoulders. "I guess that explains your reluctance to take a bath." He ducked as the man took a swing at him, and sprinted up to the bank to where they had left the horses.

******

The cook was up to his elbows in flour when Belden rode in, pounding away at his biscuit dough. He waved in greeting, pausing to scratch his nose, the flour leaving a white coat on his tobacco stained mustache. "That didn't take you so long," he observed.

Belden swung down from his horse, pinching a piece of the sourdough. "Some benevolent soul built us a prairie bridge, chutes and all." He chewed on the wad of dough awhile, and then swallowed. "All we have to do is patch it up, get…" The man stopped mid-sentence, his eyes on the interior of the wagon. Toby's impression was still imprinted in the bag of flour, but it was clear the kid was gone. "When did he leave?" He asked the question as if it was the cook's fault the boy was no longer there.

Eli was having none of it. "I cook," he announced, "I don't tend the babies."

Belden heard a cough behind him, and closed his eyes. The coughing got louder. Hands knotted at his hips, he turned around. Charlie was grinning at him like some monkey in a cage, his hand extended, the fingers waggling. Trace dug into his pocket and pulled out a double eagle, pressing it into the man's open palm. The foreman tipped his hat in thanks and headed for the picket line. Trace could see his shoulders shaking in silent laughter as he unsaddled his horse. "Toby's pony. He took the mare out on his own?" He turned back to the cook, his finger pointing to the empty place in the string of horses.

Eli avoided Belden's eyes, intent on his biscuits. "No."

Belden waited for the man to say something – anything – more. When it didn't happen he tried again, his voice soft, the words edgy. "All right; he wasn't alone. Do you know who he's with?"

The old man rolled his shoulders. "Lon." Then, sensing Belden's growing displeasure over his one-word answers, he relented. "Lon got Cully to take his place with the cows, then he came over here and rooted around in the gear. Next think I know, he and the kid are gone."

Belden dug into the side of the wagon, searching for his bedroll. His fingers closed around the coarse material, and he hefted it, cursing. Lon's pistol was gone.

The cook began shaping his biscuits, patting them into small mounds. He pressed the balls into a heavy skillet, and covered them with a damp cloth. "Didn't neither one of

them figure on you bein' back until sometime after dark,"
he said. "They're going to be surprised as all Holy Hell to
find you're already here."

Belden said nothing, thinking of the missing pistol
and the twenty dollars he had just donated to Fletcher. He
turned on his heel and led his mount to the far side of the
picket line, more aware than before of the missing pony.

******

The crew was in line for supper when Toby and Lon rode
in, the men growing silent as they watched the pair strip
their mounts and stake them out. Neither boy noticed
Trace's horse back among the string, and they headed for
the cook wagon. They each picked up a tin plate, taking
their place at the end of the line; poking and punching at
each other, their bantering loud and raucous.

Belden was beside the wagon, in the shadows on the far
side, a cup of coffee in his hand. He watched silently as the
line slowly progressed, the two truants getting closer. As
soon as Toby held out his plate, Trace called out to him and
stepped out of the darkness. "Toby." Startled, the boy looked
up from his dish. Immediately, he stepped back a full pace,
colliding with Lon, his back pressed tight against the older
boy's chest. Belden approached them both, determined to
keep his words private. "I want to talk; to both of you."

"We ain't had our supper." Lon's words were as soft as his
brother's. He placed his hand on Toby's shoulder, holding him
in place. Expectantly, he held out his own tin. Eli took the plate
and looked over his shoulder to where Belden was standing.

Trace shook his head. He pointed toward the darkness
beyond the wagon. "Get your butts over here, now!!" he
ordered. He waited for them, turning to lead the way to a

cluster of rocks, out of sight of the others. Both boys in front of him, he sat down. "I told you to stay in the wagon, Toby. I want to know why you didn't."

The kid's shoulders lifted in a silent *I don't know.*

Belden cursed the boy's stubborn silence. "Toby," he breathed. He didn't finish. There wasn't anything to say that hadn't been said earlier. Reaching out, he pulled the boy across his knees and paddled his behind; hard. When he felt the kid had enough, he set him upright on the ground in front of him, trying hard to overlook the tears. "You get back to that wagon, Toby; get your bedroll spread out, and get in it. And you stay there." The kid retreated a step, rubbing his rump. He started to bawl, loudly, and then bolted for the wagon.

Lon started after the boy, passing in front of his brother. He was grinning, the corners of his mouth twitching. Trace reached out, his fingers biting into the muscle of the youth's upper arm. "You heard me tell him that I'd paddle him, Lon." He dug his fingers deeper into the kid. "Why, Lonny? Why'd you tell him he could go?"

"It was his choice!" Lon answered, his fingers prying at the older man's hand. "He wanted to go."

Belden tightened his grip. "Like you wanted to take the pistol." He held on as the youth tried again to pull away.

"It's mine!!" Lon faced the man, his jaws set. "You treat me like I'm some snot-nosed kid!" He slapped at the pistol with his free hand. "It's mine, and I'm going to wear it!" His chest was heaving, the vein at his temple throbbing. "You want to play daddy," he tried again to pull free, "then do it. With Toby! But you get off my back!!"

Belden's hand darted out, jerking the gun belt from the boy's waist. "I've never been on your back, boy; and you better hope to God I never am," he declared. He dropped the pistol and belt to the ground at his feet. His fingers relaxed and he eased his hold on his brother. "You hired Cully to ride your spot. Now you can ride his. Night watch, eight to midnight." He stooped down and picked up the gun belt, buckling it and looping in over his shoulder.

Lon backed up, his fingers rubbing at the soreness in his upper arm. "I've got the midnight to four spot!" he shouted.

Belden shook his head. "You've got them both," he corrected.

"No!!"

Trace grabbed the kid with both hands, one hand on each shoulder. He shook him; hard. "There isn't a man on this crew that tells me no when I give him an order. Not one. And you aren't any different from the rest!! You'll ride when I tell you to ride, sleep when I tell you to sleep…"

"…and draw my wages when I'm' sick of it and want out? " Lon bucked against the hands that held him, breathing hard. It was a futile gesture, his brother a full head taller and considerable pounds heavier.

Belden drew his right arm back, his hand open. He caught himself mid swing, the hand hovering in the air and then dropping limp to his side. He inhaled, holding his breath a long time as he fought the anger back to the pit of his burning stomach. When he spoke, the rage was still in his voice. "You get your rear end out there." He jabbed a finger in the direction of the circle of firelight. "Get yourself a fresh mount, and get to work." He stared into the boy's face for a long time, his breath hot against the kid's flushed cheeks. "Now, Lon," he ordered, the words coming through clenched teeth. He wrapped his fingers around the boy's arm, roughly shoving him in the direction of the picket line. He watched after the boy along time, a dull ache growing at the back of his head.

Charlie moved out from the darkness beyond the rocks and handed Belden a cellophane wrapped cigar he'd been hoarding since Liberty. "When you finished with Toby, you should have beat Lon's tail end," he observed, no longer caring if he was trespassing.

Belden accepted the smoke, and lit up. "He's fifteen, Charlie. *Fifteen*!" He was quiet a moment. "I wasn't much older than that when Pa died," he said, remembering. "I had a ranch to run, three brothers to raise…" He flicked the ash off the end of the cigar. "We were at war with the Comanche!"

"Different time then, Trace." Fletcher had lost his family to the raiders. His voice turned gravelly, and he cleared his throat. "We all grew old fast in those days. Now…" Charlie's thoughts began to drift again, until he slammed the doors on the old hurts, on the past. "Lon's a kid, a snot-nosed kid.

"We've spoiled him, Trace. All of us." He coughed. "He's never had to share you. Not with a woman," he chose he next words carefully, "not with some kid."

"Toby," Belden said, reading the man's thoughts.

"Toby," Charlie repeated.

"Well, that's just too bad." Trace turned his head toward his foreman. "If he can't get along with Toby, then just how you think he's going to get along with Adam if…"he corrected himself, "…*when* Adam comes home."

Fletcher was shaking his head. "He won't." He chewed on his smoke, looking like a man with a great deal on his mind, and even more that he wanted to say. "It's going to happen, Trace. Lon's going to keep pushing, and…" He changed his mind about speaking the rest of his piece, and let it drop. "Goodnight, Trace."

Belden followed the man back to the campsite, stopping at the chuck wagon to retrieve his blankets. He could hear the sound of Toby's quiet sobbing. It didn't seem that he had hit the boy that hard, and yet… Cursing silently, he shook out his blankets, spreading them beneath the wagon.

When he laid down, he made himself a silent promise. The next time he picked up a stray, it was going to be some hound; some old dog he could scratch behind the ear when he felt so inclined; toss a bone. *Cart out into the woods and shoot when it got too troublesome.*

He tried laying on his back, and then his side, finally shifting to his stomach, using his arms for a pillow. That was even worse. The last time he had slept on his stomach was after his old man had walloped him for helling around with Charlie Fletcher. He wondered if Toby was sleeping on his belly.

He began to drift off, into that pleasant limbo before the dreams. There was sound above him, like the noise of mice scurrying in the rafters of the old house, and he opened his good eye, thinking it a dream. The scratching sound continued, pieces of dirt falling about his head, dropping from the bottom of the wagon. "Trace?" a voice whispered.

"What?"

"You still mad at me, Trace?"

Belden had to think about that, remembering the twenty dollars the kid's contrary little hide had cost him, recalling the grin on Charlie's face when he collected. "No," he said finally.

There was a long silence, and then the sound of the kid sniffling. "Trace?"

"What now?"

"Can I sleep with you?"

That, Belden didn't have to think about. "Get your gear together and get down here," he ordered gruffly.

It took the kid less than a minute, and then he was back where he belonged; where he'd slept from that first night, his head tucked under Belden's chin and his back up against the man's belly. "Goodnight, Trace," he whispered, yawning.

Belden pulled the blanket up around the boy's shoulder. "Goodnight, son." He said the word without realizing it.

CHAPTER 10

———

Charlie stood close to the fire, rubbing his hands to get the blood started. He watched as the other men drew cards, to see which ones would play dam builders and which ones would tend to the cattle. Those who were to remain behind proved poor winners. They let loose with a chorus of catcalls, hooting their own personal brand of insults as the losers drew their shovels from the supply wagon and started off. The foreman squared his shoulders and turned to face the younger Belden, tapping him on the shoulder. "You're going with me, Lon," he announced.

Lon shook his head. "No."

Fletcher pulled on his gloves, easing the leather in place between his fingers. "You know the trouble with you, Lonny?" He didn't expect an answer, and didn't wait for one. "When Trace got done whalin' the kid's behind last night, he should have doubled over that fancy gun belt you're so proud of, and beat your rear end." Satisfied with the gloves, he knotted his hands at his hips, his eyes on the crew. "Only thing is Trace feels you're too grown up for that kind of daddyin'.

"Now, me," Fletcher continued, turning to face the youth, "I'm not so sure. You give me any trouble, and like as not, I'll beat the Hell out of you with a doubled lead rope."

The boy's eyes narrowed as he considered the man's warning. "Trace," he said. "He told you to take me along."

"That's right, boy." Fletcher finished a final cup of coffee. "Trace figures that if I keep you busy workin', you won't feel so inclined to go runnin' off again. Don't push him, Lonny," the man cautioned. "Or me."

Lon heaved his empty mug into the dirt beside the fire. He mounted the black gelding he'd ridden the night before, raking the animal's side with his spurs as he kicked the horse into a run; purposely cutting close to the spot where Trace stood.

Belden held his ground as the kid passed, his pant legs spattered with mud and cow droppings as the horse brushed by him. The jeering catcalls of the cowhands continued, urging the construction crew forward, and Belden raised his hand. He waved the men into silence. "All right, gentlemen," he shouted, "let's get theses cows up and moving!" He slapped his gloves against his thigh, and the 'punchers fell in behind him, moving to the picket line.

The cattle moved out a crawl, lazy, their bellies full of water and grass, lethargic under a rising sun. White steam rolled off their backs, and they complained loudly as they were kicked and prodded along the bank. Toby was with Belden, riding point, full of his usual morning euphoria.

"You take care of Solomon this morning, Toby?" Belden asked.

The kid nodded. He was singing, tunelessly, bits and pieces of the words drifting above the sloshing plod of the Herefords. The longer and harder Belden listened, the more sure he was of one fact: the little ditties the kid sang were not the sweet *Jesus Loves Me* Sunday-go-to-meeting hymns a boy usually learns at his Mama's knee. "That's enough, Toby." Belden leaned forward in his saddle and tapped the kid's shoulder.

Toby faced him, a look of injured innocence radiating from the blue eyes. "Lon says the cows like music," he smiled, contrite. He started singing again, louder, watching the man out of the corner of his eye.

Belden wiped a gloved hand over his face. For some reason he didn't understand, the kid seemed intent on testing the limits. He decided the best course of action was to simply ignore the boy; to allow him to get whatever it was out of his system. It seemed like a sensible solution. On his best day, Toby had the attention span of a honeybee, flitting from one splash of color to the next in a persistent search for something sweeter.

They rode on for a time, the kid's volume steadily increasing, the songs becoming more raucous. Trace continued to ignore the boy: until the lyrics began detailing the adventures of a lady of leisure, and the dimensions of a certain portion of her anatomy and its use. "Cully!" Belden grabbed the cheek strap on the little mare's bridle. He pulled her to an abrupt stop, almost unseating the boy, waiting for Cully to take their place. Then he led the kid's pony to a grove of scrub pine on the riverbank, and dismounted.

Reaching up, he pulled the kid off the pony, wrapping his arms tight around the boy's upper body when the youngster began to fight him. Toby kicked and clawed, pulling an arm free to punch at the man's back and shoulders. He began to scream. One swear word after another. Belden his hands were now gripping the boy's upper arms, just below the shoulders. "Stop it, Toby." He shook the kid. "I said stop it!!" When there was no response, he eased the boy to the ground and swatted him across the rear. The struggling stopped.

The kid stood before Belden, his head down, his small chest rising. Then, suddenly, he grabbed the man's legs. "I don't want to go back, Trace!" He buried his face against the man's stomach. "*I don't want to go back!!*"

Belden stood rock still, his open hands suspended above the boy's shoulders. "Toby…"

"Please, Trace," the kid begged. He lifted his head, his face streaked with tears, his nose running.

Trace dug into his pocket for his handkerchief and handed it to the boy. He forced himself to think of his son, Adam, and what the consequences would be if he didn't return Toby to Liberty. But when he closed his eyes to concentrate on that thought, to form a mental picture of his son, the only image that came was Toby. He reached out, his hand on the boy's head. Impulsively, he pulled the kid close and held him, for a long time.

"Charlie says we need more help at the causeway." Lon's voice cut into the quiet sound of Toby's crying. He was above them on a small sandstone ledge, his expression grim. His back was ramrod straight, and he looked like a cat poised at a mouse hole. The black gelding sensed his mood, and the animal was dancing, fighting the bit, pieces of yellow gravel cascading down the side of the draw.

Belden nodded, reading the look on the boy's face, the anger behind the eyes. "We'll be there," he said. He watched as the youth whipped the black's head around, shaking his head when Lon gouged the horse's sides with his spurs. He wondered how long Lon had been on the ledge, what he had seen and heard. "We've got work to do, Toby," he said. Grabbing the boy by the collar and the seat of his britches, he hoisted him up on the pony.

They joined the others, taking up a position at point, encouraging the cows to move at a faster pace, the only noise the comforting creak of leather and the steady, soft plodding of split hooves against sand. There was an occasional whistle from one of the outriders as they pushed the herd even harder. It took them the majority of the day to make the long drive to the causeway. Belden sent the boy forward to help the cook set up the new camp site, and then made the circuitous trip around the outer edge of the herd, issuing orders, pointing out the pasturage in the basin that converged at the mouth of the prairie bridge. He gave the same speech to each man. "Keep them bunched, pack 'em in. We're going to need some more men to work on that causeway." The last was greeted by with the same low groan of displeasure.

Lon was on the causeway, ankle deep in the water, his shirt wet at the back and armpits; his face flushed. Trace moved to help him, straining against the makeshift lever as they pried a large rock into place at the lee side of the mud mound. Trace dug his heels in and held onto the pole as Lon bent down and used a hand sledge to drive in the retaining stakes. When they finished, Belden reached out to help Lon to his feet. "Good job, Lonny." The compliment fell on deaf ears.

Charlie was at work just ahead of them, driving his own set of stakes. He lifted his eyes quickly to Belden, and then shifted them back to the hammer. "Next time you buy any cows," each word was accompanied by a blow from the heavy sledge, "you make sure you got a spur track runnin' right up to the back door of the ranch!" He started on a second post, the sweat beading on his forehead.

There was a splash, the noise followed by the loud yells of good-natured laughter that drowned out the words of the unhappy 'puncher. Lon stopped his hammering, offering his own words of sympathy. "Taggert, you dumb jackass!" he yelled, watching as the man clambered back up on the causeway. "You're supposed to feel your way with that pole, not drag it behind you!"

Four more cowhands waded onto the bridge, sloshing their way past the foreman and Belden, buckets of dirt and gravel in both hands. Trace stood aside, measuring the distance between the repair crew and the opposite bank. "How much longer, Charlie?"

Fletcher hammered in his last stake. "We should be able to start movin' them across first light tomorrow." He stood up, pausing to wipe at his forehead. "Must have been one hell of an outfit that came through here," he mused. "You can bet it took them more than a day to throw this up." He studied the causeway for a long time.

Belden nodded in agreement. "Lockheart, maybe, or one of the other big spreads on the border." He stroked his chin. "We won't see any more big drives, Charlie," he said with a degree of regret. "Not like after the War." He snorted in disgust. "There aren't going to be that many big spreads, either. Not with the dirt farmers claiming so much range land."

"Well, it was fine while it lasted." Charlie grinned up at the man. "Just as well, too," he opened his hands, displaying the large blisters on his palms.

Belden eyed the man, the ghost of a grin forming at the corners of his mouth. "I'll tell Eli to fix something special for all you hungry dirt-grubbers. Potato soup, a nice vegetable pie. A stewed chicken, maybe." He was laughing when he said the words.

"I may have to work like a sodbuster, Trace, but I sure in hell don't plan on eating like one!! You tell Eli to butcher the fatted calf, his wandering boy is coming home!" The foreman waved Belden away, the salute turning into an obscene gesture.

The work continued far into the afternoon, the men dragging into camp at twilight, too tired to complain. They sat huddled around the fire, puncturing the crop of blisters that had sprouted on their palms and fingers. Toby made the rounds with the coffee pot, solicitous and properly sympathetic. He trotted to the end of the bridgework, to the place where Belden and the foreman stood surveying the repaired causeway, filling their cups. Belden reached out, ruffling the kid's hair. "You want to take a ride, Toby?" He nodded toward the opposite shore. There was still enough light to make the ride.

"He….ck, yes!" The kid was elated, grinning up at the man.

"Then go get the bay. We'll double up." Belden watched as the kid sprinted back to the cook wagon.

"He's still talkin' to you," Charlie said, rubbing at the ache in the small of his back.

"He is," Belden replied. He pointed toward the fire, to the place where Lon was sitting. "He isn't." He handed the foreman his cup and took the reins of his gelding from the boy. Climbing aboard, he pulled Toby up behind him. "Hang on, sprout. We're going to take a look at what's on the other side of this river."

Charlie watched after the pair, a cup in each hand. Out of the corner of his eye, he could see Lon, the kid's gaze riveted on Belden and the boy. The foreman bunched his sore shoulder at the sudden chill that swept his back and neck, an uncomfortable feeling deep in his gut that refused to go away. He kicked at a frog that was eyeing him from the bank and cursed. There was going to be more trouble before the drive was over. Big trouble.

******

They rolled out at four in the morning, the night riders pausing just long enough to grab breakfast and a fresh mount before riding back to the cattle. Charlie was already in the saddle, as was Belden. The two men sat on their horses at the beginning of the submerged passageway, staring across into the grey haze at the other side of the river. One by one, a series of hanging kerosene lanterns twinkled on, zigzagging across the water. They looked like the *lamperas* that lined the streets of the Nuevo Laredo during *La Posada*, the lights marking the way with an eerie yellow-white shine. Trace turned his bay and headed toward the cook wagon. He reached out, placing a hand on Eli's shoulder. "We'll get you started across. This wagon first, and then the supply wagon." He glanced toward the rear of the wagon. "Where's Toby?"

"Said he was going to ride across on the pony," the cook answered.

"No he's not." Trace disappeared into the gray dawn and when he returned, the boy was with him. He unloaded the kid, watching as he took his seat beside the cook. "You watch the wagon on your side, Toby. You've got about six inches," he measured the distance with his hands, "between the wheels and the edge of the causeway. You make sure you let Eli know if you get too close to the edge." He made it sound like he was giving the kid a load of responsibility, his tone serious. "You keep an eye on Solomon, too," he reminded, pointing to the tethered yearling.

"We're ready, Trace." Charlie pulled up beside Belden, pointing to the arc of light coming from the other bank, a lantern swinging back and forth above the mist.

Belden nodded. "Then let's go." He moved to the head of the team, leading the way into the chute at mouth of the causeway. The bay hesitated, nervous, stopping at the water's edge to paw at the vapor that layered above the water. Trace spurred the animal in the side, and then used the quirt, the horse moving reluctantly into the river.

Behind him, the heavy draft horses moved obediently onto the causeway, the wagon swaying slightly, then lurching forward. The wheels dug into the mud, lifting compacted rings of yellow clay as they turned, the mud plopping loudly as it shook free from the metal rims.

Both wagons made the crossing without incident, two wranglers following with the *remuda*. The lead group pulled up on a ridge overlooking the river, Charlie and the kid helping to string the new picket lines.

The sun was just lifting its face into the grey sky, the horizon streaked pink and gold. Belden recrossed the causeway a final time, extinguishing and collecting the lanterns as he went. He remained mounted, looking to the hills, watching with pride and satisfaction as the cows began moving in a slow stream toward the chute, funneling toward the crossing. The animals moved three abreast, Fletcher roping a belled cow and pulling her into the water. The remainder began to follow the animal like lambs being led by a Judas goat, moving in a steady line toward the opposite bank.

Eight hundred fifty head of cattle moved across the earthen bridgework, a sea of chestnut and white above the green-blue swell of the water. The split hooves cut into the packed earth and rocks, the water churning a yellow grey beneath the fat bellies, the cows following one after the other, the basin emptying. From his vantage point on the ridge above the river, Belden continued to watch. It was like seeing a huge hourglass emptying, red sand flowing from one part to the other, trickling down through the narrow channel in the middle.

It took a full day to move the cows, the drive stopping once, at noon, as the crew was forced to shore up small breaks in the causeway. The men resumed the drive, cursing and cajoling both their mounts and the bovines;

angry because the forced delayed had denied them their noon meal. Finally, the last group of cows crossed the submerged land bridge; just as the cook hollered for the crew to come and get it.

And then the sky opened up, and it began to rain.

CHAPTER 11

———

The storm blew in from the northwest, sweeping down out of the mountains without any warning. The air became deathly still; warm. And then the wind began, a sudden shift in the temperature. Stunned, they stared into the wind and saw the churning thunderheads rolling a wall of water towards them, Belden's shouted warning torn from his lips and hushed by the roar of the wind. The tarp covering the supply wagon tore loose and began snapping, the brass grommets striking the sides of the wagon and popping against the wood like a string of Chinese firecrackers. Suddenly, the canvas billowed out like a sail. Lon kicked his horse in the ribs, forcing the animal close to the wagon, Trace behind him.

The wind shifted, and the canvas reversed its direction, snapping loose at one corner. Lon's black reared straight up as the tarp cracked loudly and stung its face. The animal pawed wildly at the air, fighting the thing that continued to slap at its head and chest; the horse suddenly going over on its back. Lon jumped free just before the animal hit the ground, landing on his feet, and ran for the wagon.

Toby was there, his small hands groping for the fluttering canvas. He caught an edge with both hands and hung on, lifted off his feet and the wind again changed direction and tore through the wagon in the opposite direction. The tarp lifted even higher, tearing the boy off his feet a second time as the wind whipped underneath the heavy cloth and it stood out like a banner over the side of the wagon.

Belden grabbed the boy around the waist and lifted him onto the nervous bay. "It's all right, son." He held him for a long time, feeling the boy's heartbeat throbbing against his chest, and then set him back on the ground. Using the bay as a windbreak, Belden watched as Lon and Toby fought the cloth back into place; Lon retying the straps that secured the heavy tarp to the wagon's frame.

The sky was growing darker, the wind intensifying. Rain poured across them like scalding water, cutting their cotton shirts from their arms and shoulders. The men struggled with their slickers, riding and dressing at the same time, heading for the cattle. The cold increased, robbing the men and animals of their body heat as it began to hail. Nugget sized chunks of ice pelted against the rubber ponchos, beating against the metal smokestack on the cook wagon, the relentless clatter of frozen rain spooking the cows even more than the howling wind. The cattle at the center of the herd started to mill, the wet hides a maroon whirlpool that began spreading, the circle of movement growing, spiraling toward the animals on the outer edges.

They broke. The run started on the far side of the camp, the animals fleeing the sound of the hail and the wind. The men rode instinctively, forming a ragged line behind the herd, following the cattle as they stampeded across the windswept prairie.

Trace kicked his horse into a sloshing run and pulled his

rifle from its scabbard. He fired into the air, three times in rapid succession, and heard an answering report on his right. The pattern was picked up by the others, and Belden located his riders by the sounds. Cully was just ahead of him, the boom of his .54 caliber Sharps carbine competing with the thunder, and he could hear the sharp crack of Fletcher's small-bore pistol to his left. Rifles and handguns continued their barking, competing with the wind. They drove forward, running their horses in a useless attempt to keep up. It seemed as if they ran for miles.

Then, as suddenly as the storm had begun, it ceased. The rain swept across the river in a great arc-shaped wall, beating the swollen waters into submission. Belden pulled the gelding to a stop, the animal's side heaving, patches of thick white lather on its neck and shoulders. A great shudder coursed through the bay's body, its front legs buckling. The horse went down to its knees, and with a sudden surge of effort, pushed itself back up on all fours. It stood there, front legs splayed, as if knowing that if it fell again, it would never get up.

Lon pulled up beside Trace, his face pale. "Well, at least they're running in the right direction." He wiped the back of his hand across his forehead and drew it away, a bright smear of red staining his knuckles.

Belden stretched a sore arm across the narrow gap that separated them, turning the boy's face toward him. He exhaled, seeing white bone, fighting the worry in his voice. "You've got a gash in your forehead, Lon," he said with a forced calm. He reached into his pocket for his bandanna, cursing when he withdrew the wet rag.

Lon nodded, fingering the growing knot as he pressed the damp cloth against the wound. "Jeez, Trace," he said. "I never even felt it…" He slumped forward, suddenly sick to his stomach.

Belden moved the bay closer, his arm around the boy's shoulders. He watched as the other riders converged in a half-circle, and nodded at Lon. Searching the faces, he settled on Fletcher's second-in-command. Carefully, he appraised the man's horse. "Cully," he said softly. "You ride on ahead. Tell Charlie we're coming in, and that Lon's been hurt." The cowboy nodded, his brow creasing as he saw the blood clotting on the boy's cheek. He jerked his horse around, applying his quirt.

Charlie was waiting for them. He watched as Trace helped Lon from his horse, pointing to the upended keg beside the open tailgate of the supply wagon. His kit was laid out; rolls of cotton bandages, a half-dozen assorted probes and glass bottles and vials carefully arranged. Together, he and Trace eased the boy onto the makeshift stool.

He uncorked a fresh bottle of whiskey, covering Lon's eyes with a cloth as he doused the cut, the liquor burning deep into the boy's skull. Lon lifted his hand in protest, swallowing against the tears that were forming, faking a bravado he did not feel. "Give me that bottle!" He grabbed the jug and hoisted it to his lips as he took a long swallow.

"He's going to need stitches, Trace." He spoke directly to Belton, and then addressed the youth. "Stitches, Lon."

The kid took another long drink from the bottle. The whiskey was already working. "Keep it neat, old man," he ordered. "There's a hundred women in Laredo going to be broken-hearted if you mess this up." He tilted his head back onto the man's knees and shut his eyes, his hands firmly locked around the neck of this whiskey bottle.

Expertly, the foreman set about repairing the deep gash on Lon's forehead. Carefully, he gathered the torn skin, patting it back into place. The tear was longer than he first suspected, and well into the hairline. "Get his hands,

Trace," he ordered. He picked up a cake of yellow soap, the bar filled with metal spines of various sizes, and selected one of the smaller needles. He worked it back and forth in the soft bar for a time before he withdrew it. "It's going to hurt some, Lonny," he warned. Deftly, he poked his finger into a saucer of whiskey at his elbow, and withdrew a shaft of horse tail hair that had been soaking. He threaded the needle, and then, taking a breath, he began.

Belden held onto Lon's arms, just above the wrists, forcing them back into the boy's lap. He watched as the needle penetrated the skin at the edge of the wound, Fletcher carefully pulled the edges of the torn skin together, careful not to overlap. He used his thumbs to smooth the tissue as he worked; the needle making no sound at all. The only noise was a series of soft moans as he pulled each suture taut.

Trace felt something pushing at his knees and saw the back of Toby's head appear between them. The boy took one look and then withdrew, scrambling backwards in the mud. Belden could hear him running, and then heard the sound of his retching.

Charlie finished, stepping back to admire his handi-work. "Not bad, Lonny," he said. "'Course you're going to have to explain to all those hundred women why one eye's sewed shut." He wiped his hands on the boy's shirt.

Long bolted upright, dropping the bottle of whiskey, his fingers going to his mended forehead. The other men who were watching laughed in a single voice; Lon's opinion of the camp doctor's sense of humor lost in the noise.

There was no supper that night, the men going out in parties of two, looking for strays. They found nine dead cows before there was no more light, all of the men grim-faced as they returned to camp. They turned in, searching for a dry spot to spread their wet bedrolls.

Trace laid Toby's bed out in the back of the supply wagon; right next to the pallet where Lon was already sleeping. The kid undressed quietly, crawling under the covers, his face still white. "Is it always like this?" he asked, whispering.

Belden reached into the wagon for his own bedroll, careful not to disturb Lon. "No, Toby. Sometimes it's a lot worse," he said. He pulled the blanket up around Lon's shoulders, gently touching the knot on the youth's head. Tucking his bedroll under his arm, he turned, and felt Toby's hand on his.

"Where you goin', Trace?"

Belden jerked his head in the direction of the campfire. "Out there," he said simply, pulling away.

Toby rose up on one elbow. "Why?"

"Because that's where the men are, Toby." He was quiet a moment. There were things a man needed to do, and a boy needed to learn. "The crew has been through Hell, Toby. Not even a cup of coffee since breakfast. Their clothes, their blankets, are wet; and there isn't a dry place to sleep." He faced the boy, hoping he'd understand. "I can't sleep here in the wagon, and expect them to bunk down in the mud." His face softened. "You never ask another man to do a thing you wouldn't do yourself, Toby."

"But Lon…" the boy said, nodding at the still form at his side.

"Lon was hurt, Toby. He needs sleep, and he needs to be someplace clean and dry."

The kid was pulling on his pants. "Then I'm coming, too." He picked up his blanket and boots and reached out to the man. Belden hesitated, and then lifted the kid down from the wagon. Together, they headed for the fire.

******

They slept the sleep of the dead, all of them exhausted. Charlie woke first, coming awake with the first light of day. He stretched, scratching himself as he stood up. He looked around, making a slow circle, unbelieving, and hobbled quickly across to the spot where Belden and the kid lay. "Trace," he whispered. And then, more urgently, "Trace!"

Belden rolled over, his arm asleep. He eased Toby's head down onto the blanket and sat up, adjusting the eye patch. He pulled on is boots. "What's wrong?"

Fletcher didn't answer, just made a broad sweep with his outstretched arm. Belden stood all the way up, his hands going to his hips. They were on an island.

"Holy…!" Lon was at his elbow, the kid's right eye swollen partially shut. He shook his head, his mind refusing to accept what he was seeing.

Belden looked out over the river and made a slow one-hundred-eighty-degree turn. They were surrounded by water on all sides. He looked down to the place where the causeway ended, his brows raising. The water had risen during the night, spilling around the chute, following the natural downward cleavage of the hillside, flowing around the base of the small escarpment and spreading wide into the gully before rejoining the river. He felt a sinking feeling in his chest as he saw the body of a Hereford partially submerged at the edge of the new shoreline. "We've got to get the cattle, Charlie." He could see the herd spread out on the other side of the channel, his face clouding. "Who's with the herd?" he asked, his eyes narrowing.

"Delgado," Charlie answered. "And old Poke Williams." He thought a minute. "Cully, and Will Sutton." He swung his head toward Belden. "They were holding the herd in the arroyo." He stopped speaking, watching as a ragged line of cows moved toward the water, thinking of the potholes that lay hidden beneath the new channel; the potholes and the deeps pits that had been dug when the causeway was first built.

Belden spun on his heel, angry. "I want to know why they aren't holding those cows back," he raged. He moved back into the circle of sleeping men, bending down to shake each man awake as he passed. Lon followed behind, less gentle in his efforts, toeing the men with his boot. Toby was on his feet, tagging behind.

They saddled their horses, Fletcher leading the way. He ordered the other men to wait on the bank, plunging into the chasm of water that separated them from the cattle. His horse moved through the murky stream, chest deep, cutting through the water with high-stepping mincing movements. Belden was on the bank, his gaze on the water directly in front of the foreman. He unfastened the rope from his pommel, shaking out a loop. Charlie's big grey took two more plunging leaps and then disappeared. "Charlie!!" Belden spun the rope and threw, the stiff hemp slapping against the surface of the water. Quickly, he drew in the line and threw again, this time hitting his intended mark, the loop settling over Fletcher's head and outstretched arm. The man kicked loose of his horse, disappearing under the water again as his stiff leg hung up in the stirrup. He kicked harder, gasping for air, and allowed himself to be pulled through the water, the grey scrambling up the bank and returning to the *remuda*.

The foreman dragged himself up on the embankment, his face grey as he put his weight on his crippled leg. "I knew the potholes were there," he said, out of breath, "but damned if I can tell where." He shook himself, pulling off his hat and wringing the water from his hair.

Belden called to his brother. "You get ready to rope, Lon." He recoiled his wet line and refastened it on the horn. "Toby, you go tell Eli I need that fifty-footer out of the supply wagon." The kid trotted off, Belden watching, and returned with the rope. "Get your pony. I'm going to need your help, too." The kid's face lit up like a jack-o-lantern, and he sped off to saddle the mare.

"What you plan on doing, Trace?" Lon was mounted on his sorrel, the horse skittish as he came to the edge of the water.

Belden was busy with the rope. He pulled an end free and slipped the loop over his head and one arm, rotating the rope until the *hondo* was resting on his belt at his side. "I'm going in." He pulled his revolver from his holster and tossed it to Charlie. "If I lose the horse, don't pull me out unless I give you the high sign. I'm going to try and string a guide line." He turned, seeing Toby. "I'm going to tie off to the kid's pony."

"Why the kid?" The edge had returned to Lon's voice, the resentment.

"He can't swim, Lon." Belden had no time for long explanations. "I've got enough to worry about out there," he gestured toward the water, "without wondering where the boy is." He mounted the bay and kicked the animal in the side, using his spurs; moving up to where Toby sat waiting. "You stay right here." Carefully, he knotted the end of the rope on the paint's saddle. "Watch that the rope doesn't get fouled, and don't give me any slack, unless I call for it. You understand?"

"Yes, sir. I understand." The kid nodded, his eyes wide as he stared into the swollen river.

Trace urged the bay into the water, picking a point to the right of the path Charlie had taken. He picked out a landmark on the other side of the channel, a single dead tree stump that jutted up out of the brown earth, and headed out.

The bay fought the water, Belden uncoiling the rope as he went, staring into the water ahead of him, watching for changes in color and current. He nudged the gelding, turning him slightly to the right as he came to a place in the river where the water was whirlpooling in a dark series of eddies, kicking his feet free of the stirrups when he felt the bay's hind legs begin to slide. The horse strained, pulling itself forward with his front legs, belly deep in the water. They moved on slowly, the water becoming shallower, the horse finally climbing up onto the opposite bank. Trace could hear Toby let out a whoop, and turned, acknowledging the gesture with a wave. He swung down from the bay and ducked out of the rope, securing the line to the solitary tree stump. On the other shore, Lon marked the spot where the boy's pony stood, stepping back as Fletcher hammered a picket stake into the earth. Together they fastened their end of the rope to the pike, pulling it tight.

They crossed the water single file, following the rope guideline, leading the string of horses from the *remuda*. Picketing the spare mounts away from the water, they portioned out shares of grain. Two men remained with the riding stock, the others recrossing the stream.

The two wagons had to be floated across, the wheels removed to make them flat bottomed boats. It took two teams of men, one on either side of the water, to ferry the clumsy vehicles on their voyage. Both men and animals fought the strong current. Finally, the chore was complete. They reset the wheels and positioned the wagons several feet apart. While the cook busied himself with a quick inventory of the storm damaged supplies, the hands collected firewood.

The crew set about digging a long, shallow trench between the two wagons. They filled the hole with cow chips and green branches from the scrub pines near the river. Above the pit, they stretched two lines, fastening them off to the supply wagon on one side, the cook wagon on the other. It didn't take long for the ropes to fill with blankets and wet clothes, the air heavy with the smell of steaming dung and pungent pine.

CHAPTER 12

Belden stood at the mouth of the arroyo, ankle deep in mud. He bent down, scraping away the drying mud that caked the man's body, cleansing the face. "Poke," he breathed. Tight-lipped, he pressed his fingers against the man's eyelids, closing them. "Any sign of Delgado?"

Charlie shook his head. He waved a hand at the two riders, signaling them forward, catching the rope that Cully tossed him. He set about his grim task, pulling the line tight around the front legs of the dead horse. He repeated the chore, fastening the second rope to the hind legs, and then stepped away. "Hell of a way for a man to die, Trace." Helpless, he watched as the dead horse was pulled away from the fallen rider.

"Can't tell if he was caught in a flash flood, of if he was up there and the side gave 'way." Belden stared up the embankment, rubbing his chin, noting the fresh scars on the bank, naked bush stems poking out from the ledge; the tiny feeder roots torn away. His eyes swept the length of the draw, settling on a mound of mud on the far side. "Charlie," he said, pointing to the slide.

They walked the small canyon, approaching the mound with a feeling of dread. Belden went down to one knee, reaching out to probe at a patch of smooth brown. "Delgado," he breathed. He dug in the muck, exposing a buckskin gloved hand, the fingers closed tight around a braided *reata*. He tugged at the line, watching the mud ridged up as he pulled the rope toward him. It was like watching a miniature gopher tunneling through the earth. About twelve feet of line was all, the rope snapped and frayed at the end.

"What do you think, Trace?" Charlie was above him, his eyes on the line.

Belden stood up, dropping the rope. "I don't know. A calf, maybe. Or trying to help Poke. God only knows."

"God," Fletcher snorted, weary. "Times like this, I don't believe there is a God; that there ever was one."

Belden nodded in silent agreement, understanding. It had been that way in the War, when he'd seen so many men die. *And for nothing*, he thought. *When you lose, all the dying is for nothing.* "Let's get him out of here, Charlie." He bent back down, trying hard to forget that Delgado had a wife and a brand-new daughter.

"Boss," Cully's voice cut into Belden's bitter remembrances. He lifted his hand, a mud-soaked garment hooked on his bent fingers. "Poke's," he said. He fanned the vest open and punched his finger through a single hole in the back.

Belden reached up to the man, taking the leather vest. Charlie was at his shoulder on his blind side, a set of arms without a body. Trace held the garment out to the man. "Rifle," Fletcher said, moving so that Trace could see him fully.

"Bishop," Trace said softly. He tossed the vest back to Cully. "Get back to camp, pick a couple men…"

"Me," Cully said, interrupting. He stared down at Delgado's premature grave. Swinging his gaze back to Belden, he spoke again. "That could have been me, Mr. Belden.

"I'll find them," he promised. He swung his horse around and headed back down the small canyon, gesturing for Will Sutton to join him.

Fletcher and Belden worked at fashioning twin travois, fastening the wheeless stretchers behind their mounts. Silently, they loaded the bodies of their two fallen comrades on the blankets. They made the long ride back to camp without speaking, both men locked within the invisible prisons of their own grief. Poke Williams had been with Belden's father, had been on the ranch for as long as Trace could remember; an ageless weather-beaten old man whose looks never seemed to change. It was as if he had been born a cantankerous old man.

Delgado. He had just appeared one morning: hungry, bare-footed. Fletcher had given him a meal, and four hours later found him still working on the woodpile. They had needed men who could work, who were willing to work. Over the objections of the others, Charlie had hired the Mexican. He never had any reason to regret his decision.

Charlie swore, his foul mood increasing as he realized the manner in which the two men had died. Poke had been shot in the back. On closer examination, they had found a hole in Delgado's belly. Close range: the powder burns still on his shirt. As if he had been interrupted during his chores and simply dispatched like a troublesome varmint. "Bastards!" The single word came with an intensity that exploded into the morning quiet, flushing a covey of prairie hens.

******

Cully was already in camp when Trace and Fletcher rode in with the bodies. He was on foot, three men trussed and huddled around the fire. Nodding his head, he pointed at the trio.

Belden dismounted, handing the reins of his gelding to the cook. Together, he and Charlie approached the three men. "Get 'em on their feet," he ordered tersely.

Cully did as he was told, aiming his boot at the stomach of the man nearest the fire. The two others jumped to their feet without his encouragement.

Belden made a slow circle around the three, his single grey eye sweeping their faces, never blinking. He watched as they followed him with their eyes, purposely stopping behind them so they could no longer see his face. He said nothing, just stood at their backs, the sound of his measured breathing cutting the air like a cold wind. One of the men began to sweat, the perspiration beading on his neck at his hairline, rolling from the creases behind his ears. Belden pulled his revolver, cocking the piece. He shoved the barrel against the bone that protruded behind the sweating man's ear, watching as the man's knees buckled and his throat contracted. "Who?" he demanded, his voice whisper quiet. He nudged the man's head with the pistol.

"Bishop!!" the man replied quickly. He moved his head forward, unable to get rid of the weight and the feel of the revolver's cold barrel. "He told us to follow you, scatter the herd when we got the chance."

"Untie them Cully," Belden snapped. He uncocked the pistol and shoved it back into his holster, the metal making a sound as it slid against the stiff leather. "Lon, get some matches from the cook wagon."

Lon's brow furrowed, and he was slow to move. Still not understanding, he did as he was told. He dog trotted back to the clutch of men, handing the match sticks to his brother. Out of the corner of his eye, he could see Eli hustling Toby into the wagon. He turned back to Trace, watching as the man turned his back on the three strangers.

When he turned around again, he had the three match sticks in his balled fist, the blue tips even.

The three intruders stood rubbing their wrists, uneasy under the sullen scrutiny of the full crew. They could feel the push at their backs, and felt a growing panic as they realized the circle had grown tighter.

Belden held out his hand. He nodded at the matches. "The man who draws the long stick takes a message back to Liberty," he said.

In turn, the three drew. The last man, the sweater, had the unbroken stick. "What's the message?" he croaked, his mouth dry.

Belden ignored the question. He jerked his head in the direction of the other two riders. "You three been together for some time?" he asked.

The man studied Belden's face. He nodded slowly. "The young one," he said, pointing to the others. "He's my kid brother. That one's a cousin. My ma's side."

Belden nodded his head, taking the man's arm. He led the way to the picket line.

Lon watched as Trace walked toward the string of horses. He turned to Cully. "What…?"

Cully nodded his head at the younger of the two riders. "Tie his hands, Lonny." He evaded the youth's eyes, busy with the other man.

Lon followed Cully's orders, pulling the rawhide thong tight around the boy's wrists. He looked up at the kid, startled by the clear blue eyes. *Like a baby's*, he thought. He eased up on the rope.

"Your old man?" the kid asked, jerking his head toward the elder Belden. A smile tugged at the corners of his mouth, and he shifted his weight restlessly on one foot.

"My brother," Lon answered. "How old are you?" he

asked suddenly.

"Sixteen," the other answered. He bunched his left shoulder and wiped his sweating chin on his shirt. "You got a cigarette?"

Lon dug into his front shirt pocket. He rolled the smoke and stuck it in the boy's mouth. It took him two tries to get the match lit.

The boy exhaled through his nose. "He as hard as he looks?" He was still staring at Belden, the cigarette dangling from the corner of his mouth.

Lon followed the other's gaze. He shrugged. "We don't get along," he said finally.

"Too bad," the boy said. He stiffened, watching as his own brother mounted and rode off.

Cully was at Lon's shoulder, his face hard. He was sweating, the dark hair at his forehead pasted against his skin. "Let's get 'em over in the shade," he said. He pointed to a decaying cottonwood on a small rise just above them.

The tree stood black against a blue, cloudless sky. The lower branches were dead or dying, the massive trunk oozing water at its base. They made the walk in silence, the dark shade enveloping them in a wet cold. Lon looked behind him and saw Trace striding toward the rise. The crew was behind him, Charlie Fletcher leading Trace's bay and Cully's dun gelding.

The boy standing next to Lon inhaled sharply. He was shaking, trying hard not to, the cigarette trembling against his lips. He gripped the butt with his teeth and took another drag, and then spit the smoke onto the ground. Deliberately, he crushed the smoldering cigarette beneath the heel of his boot.

Belden was at the foot of the tree, his eyes on the far horizon as he watched the departing rider. The man was silhouetted briefly on the skyline, and then he disappeared.

The cloud of dust that followed him billowed high into the air, dissipated and was gone. Trace turned around, his eye on the two bound men. "Cully," he called.

Cully was on the black are that was part of his personal string, and he reached down, taking the reins of Belden's bay from Charlie. He kneed his horse in the sides and led Belden's horse to where the man was standing.

Trace reached up, taking his rope from the saddle. He shook out a loop, tossing it over the head of the man nearest him; and then mounted his horse.

Lon swallowed, watching as Cully's rope snaked around the neck of the young boy standing at his side. "Trace!" He sprinted across the clearing, his hand going to the man's knee. "You can't!" He pointed a shaky finger at the boy. "He's just a kid. *Just a kid*!" he repeated desperately.

Trace shook his head. "He quit being a kid when he strapped a pistol on his hip and took Bishop's money," he said coldly. He laid his hand on Lon's shoulder. "We've got two dead men back there, Lonny," he said quietly. "Good men you've known all your life. And these two killed them," he finished.

He nudged the bay in the sides, following Cully up the small hill to the cottonwood, pulling the man behind him. Standing up in his stirrups, he tossed his coiled up and over the wide limb above his head; Cully doing the same.

"Oh, God," the oldest of the pair begged. Belden dallied his rope around his saddle horn, and nodded to Cully. Together, they jabbed their horses in the flanks, the ropes going tight. The crying stopped, the only sounds the hum of the ropes and the noise of the horses' hooves as they pawed the rocky ground at the base of the tree. Cully circled the cottonwood, twice, Belden behind him, and the two men tied off their ropes.

Lon's back was to the tree. He could still hear the whine of the ropes as they slid over the rough bark. Closing his eyes, he grabbed his churning stomach. There was another sound then, like the back and forth rocking of a child's backyard swing, the tree creaking as the limb swayed with the burden of the added weight.

The sound was still there when Cully and Charlie rode back to camp. Still there when they returned with the bodies of Poke Williams and Delgado. Even when they dug the graves for the two 'punchers, the back and forth sound of the rope cutting into the limb seemed loudest.

They buried Williams and Delgado beneath the cottonwood's cool branches. Fletcher read over them, his voice cracking as he recited the beginning of the hundred twenty-first Psalm. *I will lift up mine eyes unto the hills…*

The other two they left hanging. Belden had pinned another piece of scripture to the shirt of the tallest man. *An eye for an eye.*

******

They moved their camp, following the scattered herd, picking up the strays. A mile from where they had found Williams and Delgado, they found ten heifers bogged down in a muddy pit. The remainder of an abandoned barbed wire fence stretched for about a quarter of a mile, rising and falling with the landscape, ending – for some unknown reason – in the middle of the flooded sink. The Herefords were bawling, chest deep in the murky waters, and Belden waded into the muck, his boots making a sucking sound each time he pulled a foot free to take a step.

Two of the heifers were tangled in the wire. He reached under their bellies, grimacing when he felt the rusted wire rake across his knuckles, the inch-long barbs tearing into his skin. The smallest of the Herefords tried to get away from the man's probing hand, bucking against the wire. She stretched out, her right hind leg hung up, and Trace saw the water beneath her white belly turn bright red. "Your rope, Charlie!" He waited as the man tossed the loop, catching it in his right hand. Gently, he placed it over the animal's neck, working it around her shoulders in a straight line back to her tail, pulling it tight. Then, with the wire cutters from his back pocket, he went to work under her belly, cursing when she bucked against him. She kept lunging away from the wire, the water flushing pink a second time, and then she was free. Belden waved to the foreman, pushing and shoving the calf until she was able to get her feet under her. He stumbled through the mud after her, his hand on the rope, stopping on the bank to examine her.

The teats were torn and bleeding, and the animal tried to take a feeble step forward. Her right hind leg gave under her weight, and she lifted it, shaking as she stretched it out behind her. The blood pumped from a long tear in her underbelly, and Trace shook his head. She was bleeding to death, her eyes already beginning to glaze. The man pulled his pistol and went to her head, laying the muzzle behind her ear. He fired, and there was a soft *ooof,* the Hereford collapsing on its knees. It fell over on its side, jerking spasmodically, the legs stretching out, trembling, and then she was still.

The remaining Herefords were on the bank, pulled free by the other wranglers. Single file, they came forward, almost on tiptoe, their brown eyes seeming to pop out of their heads as they strained forward to sniff at the dead heifer. They began to low, a soft guttural sound raising on the afternoon air. It was as if the animals were in mourning.

Belden put away his pistol and took out a knife. They would eat veal tonight; fresh, expensive veal.

He loaded the butchered Hereford on the bay, the carcass gutted and smelling of blood. The gelding was skittish, turning its head to eye its burden, the horse's nostrils flaring. Belden cursed, the corpse shifted, and the bay spooked. Head down, the horse kicked out with its hind feet, pulling away from the man. Trace slammed his fist against the bay's head, between the eyes. "Charlie!"

Fletcher dismounted and went to the gelding's side. He pulled Belden's slicker from behind the saddle and wrapped the Hereford, securing the carcass in place. "You better take the grey, Trace; lead this jughead. You can send him back with one of the hands."

Belden accepted the man's offer. He swung aboard the grey, not bothering to adjust the stirrups for his long legs. Urging the horse forward, he tugged on the bay's reins, and trotted back toward the main camp.

Eli unloaded the dead beef. He jerked a thumb at the cook stove. "Fresh coffee, Trace," he said. He rolled the remains of the calf free from the slicker, dumping the carcass into the long grass beside the wagon. With an efficient agility belying his age, he set about properly dressing the Hereford.

Trace helped himself to the coffee, dosing the brew with the bottle of whiskey Eli kept stashed in the boot. He grinned, waving in greeting to Toby, watching as the boy tended the yearling bull. The Hereford was, like the boy, beginning to fill out, a broadening and thickening subtly starting to mold the features of a mature animal. *The bull would sire good calves in the years to come*, Belden speculated. Finished with his coffee, he put his cup away, and turned to unsaddle the bay.

Lon's sorrel mare was tied off at her place in the picket

line, her saddle still on her back, the cinch still tight. Belden tied the bay's reins across the line, bending down to duck under the necks of the two horses that stood between him and the mare. He reached out, disturbed by the unnatural posture of the sorrel's left front leg, the hoof cocked. He lifted her foot and cursed. There was a large rock wedged in the frog, the horse pulling away at his touch. He lowered her foot, his gaze sweeping the campsite for her owner. "Toby," he called. "Have you seen Lon?"

Toby bit his lip and cast a quick look into the shadows beside the wagon. Lon lifted a finger to his lips and shook his head. He leaned back against the wheel and took a long drag on his smoke. Toby concentrated on brushing the yearling, bending down to disappear behind the animal's shoulder. Belden called out again, louder, repeating his original question.

"You better answer him, Toby," Lon said.

"You want him to know you're here?" The kid was whispering, still raking the Hereford's thick coat.

Disgusted at the boy's dumbness, Lon exhaled loudly. "Just tell him no," he ordered.

Toby shook his head stubbornly, brushing Solomon even harder. "No. I don't want to tell Trace a lie."

"Oh, yeah?" Lon studied the kid. "Well, you better not tell him…"

"Tell me what, Lon?" Belden asked.

Toby stood up, facing the man. Belden's gloved hand was resting on the Hereford's broad back. "I got all the mud off, Trace," he said weakly, gesturing with the brush.

Lon was on his feet, his hands behind his back. He winced, pinching out his cigarette, closing a fist around the warm butt.

Belden repeated his question. "What is it that Toby better not tell, Lon?"

"Nothin'," the kid answered sullenly.

Belden raked the boy with a baleful glare. "What have you got behind your back, Lon?" he demanded. He thought immediately of the pistol. "Lon, if you've got that pistol…"

"I told you I didn't have anything!" the boy interrupted, his cheeks coloring.

"Then let's see your hands," Belden challenged.

Lon hesitated, feeling the heat on his face as he temper rose. He opened his hidden hand and dropped the half-smoked butt, then raised both arms level with his belt as he swung them to his front. Hands extended, he turned them over, exposing his palms. He felt like an infant caught pilfering from the cookie jar.

Trace eyed the boy's upturned hands, his eye narrowing as he saw the small circle of pink on the kid's right palm. He dropped his gaze to the youth's feet, jaws tensing as he spied the white-papered smoke. Disgusted – more with himself than his sibling – he took a deep breath. "I'm done, Lonny." He was determined not to lose his temper. "You get your tail over to the picket line; take care of your mare. You'll need a hoof pick and some liniment." It was getting more difficult to hold his anger in check; the boy's mulish behavior and belligerence – the tantrums and the petulance as well as downright disobedience – coming to a head. He pointed a finger a Toby. "He's half your age, and he's got more sense than you have! He takes care of Solomon," he nodded to the boy's pony, "he takes care of his horse! And he helps Eli with both teams and whatever other chores need doing. You've got four horses in the string, and they all look like hell!" He knew when he was done, he had made a mistake. Lon's eyes were filled with a bitter resentment at the comparisons, his fists clenching and unclenching, and both arms stiff at his sides.

To hell with it, he thought. Everything he had said was the truth, and if Lon couldn't live with it, then too bad. "Toby," he said. "You make sure Solomon's tied off good and proper. Then you get your pony saddled. We're going to take Charlie's horse back to him and help him look for more strays." He turned, going back to the picket line.

"What about me!?" Lon took a step after his brother, his face still red. He repeated the words, shouting. "*What about me!?*"

Belden whirled and faced the boy, pointing a long finger at him. "You're going to take care of the sorrel, like you were told." He heard the kid whisper a string of curses. "And then you're going to stay here in camp and give Eli a hand." That was the ultimate insult.

Toby checked the knot on Solomon's rope. He grinned across at Lon, tilting his head and thinking of all the times the youth had teased him about having to remain behind as cook's helper. He stuck out his tongue, and then turned to follow after Belden.

Lon stood beside Solomon, watching as his brother and Toby mounted their horses. He was sick of it; all of it. But most of all, sick of the kid. He kicked at a clump of grass, and then bent down, pushing the shoots aside. Smiling, his hand closed around the bone handle of Toby's jackknife. The same knife Trace had bought that day in Liberty.

The same day he had made Lon feel the fool; made him give the pistol back to Mrs. Cutter. He hefted the knife, bouncing it in his hand, and then snapped open the long blade. He poked out at the knot on the hitch ring, the knot securing Solomon's tether. And then he began sawing; not too much, just enough so that when the yearling got restless, when the cook was taking his nap…

******

"How many, Charlie" Belden was seated on the ground, legs crossed, his full place on his knee.

"Close to a forty head, Trace," the foreman answered, his shoulders sagging as if he were personally responsible for the losses. He toyed with his supper, stabbing at the meat.

Belden let loose a low whistle. "Well, " he said. "It could have been worse." He didn't believe it.

Lon sauntered over to the fire, his eyes on the young boy seated next to his brother. "Solomon's gone," he announced. He watched as Toby scrambled to his feet, the kid's plate spilling onto the ground. The sound of whispered cursing came to him from the circle of men. "Guess he didn't tie him off as good as he should have…" He displayed the frayed rope.

"Trace…" Toby's voice was filled with a bitter anguish. 'I tied him!"

Belden was on his feet. Unconsciously, he rubbed at a throbbing tightness at the back of his neck that was threatening to tie knots in his skull. "I know, Toby," he said softly, a tired acceptance in his voice. It was about as worse as it was going to get, and the man was tired. "It's all right."

Lon couldn't believe what he was hearing. He swallowed, the rage he felt building in his chest until he thought it would burst. "No," he said. *"No!"* This wasn't what he had planned, what he had hoped for. He threw the lead down at Belden's feet and took a step forward. "You chewed me for not taking care of a fifty-dollar horse," he shouted. "He loses a thousand-dollar seed bull, and you say it's all right!!" He grabbed Toby by the shirt front. "You were supposed to watch him, take care of him," he yelled.

"That's enough, Lon," Belden said quietly. He reached out, his hand resting protectively on Toby's shoulder. "I said that was enough." He pulled Toby back, his eyes on his brother. "Go over to the supply wagon, Toby," he said, giving the boy a push in that direction.

Lon stepped in front of the kid, blocking his way. "You know what they were saying," he started. "What everybody in Liberty was calling him?" He was shaking, his voice a quiet monotone. "Belden's bastard," he seethed. "Like he was yours. Like that bitch at the whore house…"

"Shut up, Lon," Belden cautioned, his tone matching the youth's.

Lon ignored the warning, and there was a nervous shuffling of booted feet as the crew backed away from the fire. Someone coughed and tried to stifle the sound. "You spent a lot of time away from the ranch, Trace," the boy continued. "Damned near every year since I can remember," he whispered. He was shaking even more now, the question that had been plaguing him eating at his very soul. "Is he?" he demanded. "*Is he your bastard?*"

There was a long agonizing silence, the only sound the soft sobbing of the small boy. Trace shoved him in the direction of the wagon; gently. "Eli…" he called. He waited until the old man led the boy away.

"Is he you bastard!?" Lon asked the question again, taking another step towards his brother.

Belden shook his head. "No," he said honestly. He began to smile as he realized just how important Toby had become. "He wasn't," he answered. "But he is now, Lon." He was going to keep the boy. He knew that now, knew it as sure as he knew the sun would rise in the morning.

Lon saw the determination in his brother's face; the man's intentions totally clear; too clear. "No."

"Yes," Belden answered. He bent down, picking up the lead rope Lon had thrown at his feet. He fingered the end of the rope, the unwound strands equal for the most part, the frayed edges even. "It's been cut, Lon," he said.

Lon stood his ground. "Toby," he lied.

"No," Belden said softly, sensing the lie. It was going to stop. Once and for all, here and now; it was going to stop. He dropped the lead, his hand darting out to grasp the front of Lon's shirt. He backhanded the kid, hard, his knuckles biting into the boy's soft cheek. His hand slashed through the air a second time, open palmed, and he struck the boy again. "You'll look for Solomon in the morning," he said, still holding on to the boy's shirt, "and you'll find him. Because if you don't, Lon," he threatened, the quiet words worse than the shouting, "I'm going to take that thousand dollars out of you hide. A dollar at a time," he promised.

Lon attempted to pull away, and could not; any more than he could stop the tears. He lifted a hand to the corner of his mouth, tongue and finger meeting as he tasted blood. Behind him, he could hear the mumbled approval of the men, and Charlie's whispered *about time*. Still fingering his cheek, he stared up at his brother. "In the morning," he said, fighting the tears.

Trace let go of the kid's shirt. He watched as the boy elbowed his way through the cluster of men, fleeing into the blackness beyond the fire.

CHAPTER 13

———

Eli greeted Belden with a steaming mug of coffee, the bitter brew laced with a generous shot of whiskey. Trace lifted the cup to his lips, stretching against the soreness in his lower back, taking a long swallow. He had taken the midnight to four swing, and had ridden three hours more beneath a waning full moon to search for strays. Charlie was with the cook, and he was quiet; too quiet. Trace forced a smile, hoping to improve Fletcher's mood. "I could use another cup of this," he said, holding out the tin. The smile faded as he watched Eli pour a straight shot into the cup.

"Lon's gone, Trace," Charlie said quietly. He nodded toward the string of cowponies.

Belden downed the liquor and wiped his mouth with the back of his gloved hand. "Solomon," he said. "He's out looking for Solomon."

Charlie shook his head. "He took his bedroll, jerked beef, some cash from the strong box. He's run off," he finished.

Everything, Trace knew, meant the pistol He shook his head. "We'll look for Solomon, Charlie. "Until noon. Then we're going home."

"Trace…"

Belden shook his head. "The sooner we get back to the ranch, the sooner I can start looking for Lon." He sagged against the side of the wagon, feeling tired; and old, very old. When he looked up he saw Toby. The kid was staring at him, his eyes red. Trace lifted a hand to touch the boy, feeling more pain when the kid withdrew and hunkered down in the wagon. He could hear the sound of the boy's muffled sobbing.

******

Toby waited until Belden and the others left, leading the pony away from the cook wagon before mounting her. He pulled himself aboard, checking his rope. It was his fault, all of it, just like Lon said. His fault that Lon and Trace were always fighting; just like it was his fault the Lon and Solomon were gone.

He headed toward the riverbank, backtracking the wide trail that the Herefords had left. He kept his eyes straight ahead, not wanting to see the swollen bodies that dotted the slopes above the receding river, then forcing himself to look in the fear that one of the dead animals might be the missing Solomon.

The wind ruffled the hair at his collar, and he tilted his head at a faint sound that rose and fell with the breeze. He held his breath, listening, and then kicked the mare into a trot, moving along the bank, pausing every now and then to listen.

The sound grew stronger, and Toby dismounted; leading the pony thought the tangle of driftwood and uprooted shrubs. They were ankle deep in mud now, the boy slipping and sliding his way down a gradual incline as he worked his way closer to the noise. He rounded a small bend in the riverbed, pulling up short as he almost fell into pothole.

Solomon was at the bottom of the pit, the water up even with his shoulders. He spied Toby and the mare and lurched forward, the bull calf's head disappearing beneath the water. The white snout reappeared, blowing bubbles, and then the terrified brown eyes. The struggling continued, the bull-calf sinking deeper.

"Oh, Solomon." The boy dropped to his knees beside the sinkhole, watching as the gravel on the side of the pit gave way beneath his hands. Frightened, he backed away. Still on one knee, he searched the far horizon with his eyes, and then swung his gaze back to the mired calf. The water was almost to the animal's shoulders now, his rear end completely submerged. Toby scrambled to his feet, grabbing the mare's reins.

He unfastened his rope, carefully dallying the hemp around the horn, pulling the line tight. He tested it, pulling hard, and then, slowly, began his long descent into the pit.

Solomon watched as the boy came down the side of the sink, his brown eyes wide with fear. The animal no longer struggled against the water, the muck holding him fast; the suction from the previous struggle pulling him down. The calf raised its head again, recognizing a familiar scent, drawing comfort from the boy's smell.

Toby held tight to the rope, the loop draped over his head and one shoulder. He entered the water slowly, one step at a time, his face draining of color as the water crawled inch by inch up his body. He was terrified, the large vein in his neck standing out blue-white against the pale skin, pulsing with each beat of his heart.

The water was even with Toby's armpits when he reached the calf. Solomon made a fruitless attempt to free himself, and then heaved a great sigh, relaxing. His nose was just barely above the level of the water. Toby opened his loop, pulling on the line for more slack. He lifted the rope over his head and placed it around the Hereford's neck, patting the animal and crooning softly as he worked. He pulled the loop even wider, pushing it down into the water as he leaned over the calf's back and groped for the submerged tail. He felt the matted hair beneath his fingers and lifted, running his hand out the tail's full length, the water deeper as he moved toward the animal's rear. He slipped the rope underneath the tail and pulled the loop tight. Losing his footing, he slid forward, panicking as he fell face-first into the water. He came up gulping for air, remembering the two dead punchers and their mud-soaked bodies. His fingers dug into the loose hide at Solomon's flanks. Pulling himself through the water, he grabbed onto the rope, and worked his way back to the steep bank.

His hands burned, long red lines appearing on his palms as he fought his way up the embankment. He pulled himself up over the ledge and flopped belly down at the mare's feet, his whole body shaking. He began to cry, his head buried in his arms, the fear still a big knot in his small chest. He lay there or a time, and then pulled himself up on his elbows. Behind him, Solomon let out a feeble bawl, and he turned to check the animal. Satisfied, he reached out to the mare, his arms aching as he pulled himself up into the saddle. Kneeing the horse in the sides, he turned her, urging her forward. She moved out easily at first, the slack snapping tight, the rope cutting into Toby's leg. He readjusted his position in the saddle, lifting his leg over the rope, urging her forward again. The mare dug in, her hind feet planted solidly as she strained against the Hereford's bulk; her front hooves scrabbling against the gravel. The calf began slipping backward.

Toby dismounted, scurrying back to the edge of the sink. Solomon had not been moved one mote; if anything it appeared a though he was sinking deeper. The boy trotted back to his mount, and grabbed pony's bridle; trying to pull her forward. He pulled harder, the animal fighting him as the bit pressed against her tongue. She jerked her head up suddenly, the bridle leather snapping. She bolted.

The rope unwound from the saddle horn, Toby horrified as it snaked loose, uncoiling from the pommel. The mare reared up again as the rope slapped her shoulder, and then she was gone. Ears back, mane and tail flying, she spread out into a full run, disappearing behind a far rise.

Numb, Toby watched as the lasso snaked across the ground. He ran to where the line was and grabbed, pulling hard, bracing his feet against the damp earth. Backing up, he looped the rope around an outcropping of rock, struggling to tie it off. He went back to the edge of the sink, his hands bleeding. Pulling down the sleeves of his shirt, he covered his palms with the cuffs, and started down the rope a second time. "It'll be all right, Solomon," he promised, wading into the water. He hugged the animal, his body trembling as the water closed around his chest and shoulders.

******

They backtracked the mare, grateful for the deep mud at the river's edge, her trail leading them through a maze of tangled scrub and debris. A damp fog hung above the ground, and Belden reached up, kneading the pain at his forehead above the eye patch. He'd spent a long, sleepless night, black thoughts tearing at him as he alternated between feelings of anger and the very real fear that the boy could be hurt.

"Trace," Fletcher reined in, shaking his head when Belden started to question him. "Listen," he ordered.

The sound came to them on the wind, the steady, weak lowing; close; from somewhere below them. Together, they urged their mounts ahead at a slow walk, straining to listen for more sounds. Finally, they reached the pit.

Belden hoisted a long leg over the pommel and slid to the ground beside the crater, dropping to one knee as he squinted into the grey mist rising from the brackish water. "Toby!" he called. He shouted the name, louder. "Toby!!"

There was no response, the boy chest deep in the yellow-green water, his arms around the yearling's thick neck, the calf's nose resting on his shoulder. Trace called the boy's name a third time, but it was the Hereford that reacted. The animal bellowed into the darkness, jarring the boy awake, his arms instinctively straining to lift the animal's head.

Belden wrapped a gloved hand around the rope and started down the steep incline. He waded into the hole, wrapping his arms around the kid, hefting him up against his chest. He had to unwrap the boy's clenched fingers, pry them open one by one as he pulled him away from the calf. "Charlie!!" he called out to the foreman, his right arm uplifted. Fletcher shook out his rope and made the toss. Holding Toby close, Belden wrapped the lariat around his elbow and wrist and began the climb. He could feel the warmth draining from his own body, the youngster cold and clammy against his skin.

Charlie reached out for the boy, wrapping him gently in Belden's poncho. Trace groped for the boy's feet, pulling his boots off. "I found him, Trace," the kid's words came in a weak whisper, his lips blue. He began to shake, violently, Belden's hands rubbing briskly at his feet while Charlie worked on his hands. "Tell Lon I found him…" he whispered, the voice failing.

******

For two days, the air around the supply wagon was filled with the heavy perfume of eucalyptus and camphor, a boiling kettle filling the space beneath the heavy canvas with a constant layer of steam. The moisture clung to everything, beading against the discolored tarp in shimmering droplets that accumulated, pooled and finally dropped to the floor. Only one sound came from the wagon: the rasping rattle of the boy's labored breathing.

Belden shifted in his seat, stretching his legs in an effort to ease the cramping in the long muscles of his calves and thighs. He leaned back, his fingers teepeed at his nose in a posture of constant prayer. He'd done a great deal of praying the past two days; more than ever before in his lifetime.

"Trace," the end flap lifted and Charlie poked his head inside, his eyes smarting at the heavy concentration of camphor. "They're ready…" He jerked his head toward the clearing.

Belden nodded, reaching out to adjust the blanket around the boy's thin face. He forced himself out of the wagon, and dropped to his feet from the tailgate. The sun was out, and somehow that surprised him. Bareheaded, he and the foreman walked to the place where the men were waiting. He nodded his head in a terse greeting, gesturing toward the wagon with a sweep of his hand. "I won't be riding with you," he said. "The boy…" He knew from their faces what the men were thinking and cleared his throat. "Charlie will be ramrodding the drive the rest of the way." He pointed to the wagon again. "We'll catch up with you, as soon as…" he paused, "…as soon as the boy is well enough to travel," he finished, the words filled with conviction. He refused to believe there was any other option.

There was a hesitant shuffling of feet as the crew came forward one by one, their hands outstretched. Each man in turn, shaking Belden's hand, offering him their gruff encouragement; then drifting off to their mounts.

Belden extended his hand to Fletcher, his left hand going to the man's shoulder. "Good luck, Charlie."

The foreman studied the ground at his feet for a moment, and then lifted his eyes to explore his friend's face. "I'm staying here, Trace." When Belden started to protest, Fletcher raised his hand and continued. "Cully's a good man. I've told him what's expected, and he'll get her done." He coughed and spit into the dirt, his gaze shifting to the wagon. "Yeah," he breathed. "I'm stayin' right here."

Belden's fingers tightened on the man's shoulder in a silent gesture of gratitude. Without letting go, he turned to face the crew, his gaze settling on Cully. "Take 'em home, Cully."

The young man nodded his head. "Every damned one of them, boss," he promised.

******

Their vigil was long, funereal. The boy seemed to shrink visibly while they watched, his already small features diminishing as the fever took hold and burned through his entire body. They took turns, Belding and Fletcher, swabbing the boy's cheeks and arms, first with cool water, later with a mixture of water and whiskey. And still the boy's skin burned at their touch.

He drifted, his mind regressing as he relived the unspoken horrors of an uncertain childhood. At times, he screamed as if being threatened, and then he would draw himself into a small ball, withdrawing and hiding from some unseen threat.

The childish crying was the worst, both men wanting away from the sound, yet both unwilling to leave.

One the evening of the fifth day, it became worse, the boy's frail body racked by spasms of uncontrolled coughing. Roused from a troubled sleep, Belden fell to his knees beside the boy's makeshift cot. He reached out, his massive hand on the kid's chest. He could feel the rumble beneath his palm, the wheeze echoing under the boy's breastbone. The kid's body tensed, stiffening against Belden's grasp, the cough subsiding. The rigid body relaxed, then tensed again, the boy's skin turning blue around his nose and mouth as he began gasping for air.

"He's choking, Trace!" Charlie was on his knee at the boy's head, his stiff leg protruding uncomfortably. He listened to the rattling sound deep in the boy's chest.

"Turn him on his side!" Belden ordered. He jerked the pillows from beneath the boy's head, piling them against the planking at the child's back. Pressing his head against the kid's bare chest, he held his breath, agonizing at the shallowness of the boy's breathing. "You're not going to die," he whispered. "Damn you! *You are not going to die!*" Angry, he put his left hand at the base of the kid's skull, supporting the head and neck. He used two fingers of his right hand to force the boy's mouth open, shoving one against the tongue and far back into the kid's throat. The boy struggled, gasping for air; unable to breathe. His body stiffened, his belly contracting, relaxing, contracting again. He began to cough, his chest and shoulders convulsing as he started to wretch.

Belden removed his fingers from the boy's mouth. He backed away from the cot, taking the basin Fletcher handed him and putting it under the boy's slack jaw, watching as the kid began vomiting large quantities of green phlegm and mucus. The coughing resumed, bringing more fluids, and it seemed to go on forever.

Finally the boy's body was still. Belden was wiping his face with a warm cloth, holding the child in his lap as Charlie cleaned up the cot. Fletcher spread clean sheeting across the small bed, topping the cotton sheet with a heavier blanket, while Trace removed the boy's night shirt and replaced it with a clean one. The kid was breathing easier now, the death-rattle deep in his chest quieted.

Fletcher was bathing the kid's face again. "He must have been drowning in that stuff," he tapped the full basin and the soiled toweling. "I saw blood, Trace."

Belden nodded. He had seen the flecks of red, too; and chose to dismiss them. "He's got some color now, Charlie," he took some encouragement from the fact the boy's cheeks were beginning to show a hint of pink, and that his lips were returning to a more normal hue.

"Yeah." Fletcher was unable to hide the doubt in his own voice; sorry that he could not share Belden's sense of hope. The two men sat in silence, their eyes locked on the boy's still form. It was as if they were willing the boy to heal; their efforts combining to penetrate the invisible wall that seemed to be separating Toby's frail body from his soul.

Belden stretched, unable to continue his concentration. "I've got to get out of here for a while, Charlie," he said. He pushed himself upright and, without looking back, dropped over the tailgate.

Solomon was picketed beneath the shade of a small stand of scrub oak, pulling at the grass that poked up from between the gnarled roots. Belden walked the few feet that separated the yearling from the wagon. The calf lifted its head, stretching its neck, wanting – expecting – to be scratched. Absently, Belden responded. It didn't seem right.

The calf had been in the sink with the boy, exposed to the same weather, the same wet cold. And yet the animal was thriving, becoming stronger with each passing day, while inside the wagon, the boy had grown weaker. It was almost as if the animal were somehow draining what little strength the boy had, just as the yearling had drained the heat from Toby's body that long night in the flooded pit. Belden's fingers stopped their scratching, poised at the animal's ear. His right hand dropped to his holster, and he drew his pistol.

"Don't do it, Trace! For God's sake, don't do it." Charlie reached out, his fingers an iron band around the other man's wrist.

"Look at him, Charlie." Belden thumbed back the hammer. "Like nothing ever happened…" His voice broke.

"You kill him, and all of this will have been for nothing," he chided. "The kid will have died for nothing."

Belden's face was chalk white. He eased the hammer back in place. "Charlie…?" He swung his head toward the wagon.

Fletcher relaxed his grip on Belden's wrist, shaking his head. "No, he's not gone," he said gently. "It's only a matter of time, Trace.

"I know that. You know it. You've known all along. The kid never had a prayer." Again, he was talking as if the boy was already dead.

"He's not going to die," Belden said stubbornly. He holstered the pistol, staring at the wagon. "I am not going to let him die!!"

CHAPTER 14

———

Charlie was on foot, searching the underbrush just north of the supply wagon, looking for firewood. *A week*, he seethed. *Seven days of foraging and making do; out of coffee and drinking chicory, like some dirt-scrapple sod buster.* He kicked savagely at a Gila monster, adding the small branch the lizard had been sunning on to his armload of twigs and branches.

A shadow appeared in front of him, and he heard the sound of shod hooves gently *poofing* in the sand. He straightened, shading his eyes.

"Charlie," Lon dismounted, dropping down into the sand.

"Lonny!" Charlie dropped his load of wood. The hello smile quickly faded, turning upside down in a cold frown. "Where have you been, boy?" he demanded, clamping a hand on the boy's shoulder.

"Havin' a good time," the youth lied, patting his stomach.

Charlie measured the youth with a long, knowing look. The boy's clothing was soiled and rumpled, his face pale, eyes bloodshot. He slapped the back of his hand against the kid's soft stomach; grinning with perverse satisfaction when he saw the kid wince, his eyes watering. "Fillin' your gut with cheap whiskey, playin' at being a man?" he asked, ridiculing the boy.

The youth's jaws tensed. "Where's Trace?"

Charlie busied himself restacking the supply of firewood, gathering the sticks in his arms. "You sound worried, Lon," he said, facing the youth. "Thought when you left, you made it pretty clear you didn't care one whit."

"I asked where Trace was," the boy repeated. He knotted the mare's reins around his fingers, tense.

Charlie took his time answering, pausing to scratch at the week-old stubble of red and grey whiskers that sprouted from his chin. "He's over there," he jerked his head toward the wagon, "with the kid."

"Should have figured the kid would still be around." Lon spread his legs, snapping the leather reins together. The mare was startled at the sound, her head coming up. Lon gave a vicious jerk on the reins. "I saw Solomon. Guess Trace found him without any trouble."

"You guessed wrong," Fletcher's face colored, and he heaved the carefully stacked armload of wood at the youth's feet. He poked a bony finger into the boy's chest, thumping hard as he said each word. "Toby found the calf." He balled his fist, fighting the urge to punch the boy. "The kid is sick, Lon. He's dyin'."

Lon's mouth dropped open, his face washed of color. There wasn't anything he could say. He wanted the kid out of the way, had always wanted him out of the way; but dying? "Charlie…?"

Fletcher shook his head. "Pick up the kindling. You figure on being around to watch," he said cruelly, "you can pull your own weight. Startin' now." He turned from the boy and started back down the draw. Subdued, the youth followed him, the stack of sparse kindling in his arms.

Belden watched as the pair came toward the wagon. Seated on the open tailgate, he immediately stood up. "Lon," he greeted. He allowed himself time for a long look, sweeping the boy with a restrained but reproving glance. It was clear the kid hadn't eaten, maybe for several days; and he looked in need of fresh water.

Lon dropped the bundle of wood, unable to meet his brother's quiet examination. He rubbed his hands together, brushing away pieces of bark and dirt long after they were all gone. Without looking up, he spoke. "Charlie said the bas…" he caught himself, "…the kid is sick."

Belden tensed, and then slowly relaxed. "He was," he announced, turning to direct his words to his foreman. He allowed himself the simple pleasure of a smile. "He's awake, Charlie." The smile grew. "Woke up asking for water, and now he's yelling his head off for food."

Charlie came forward, grabbing Belden's right hand in both of his. He pumped the man's hand vigorously. "Damn!" he elated. "Hot damn!!" He was shouting; the worry and fatigue easing from around his eyes.

"I'm not stayin', Trace," Lon's voice cut into the celebration.

Belden withdrew his hand from Fletcher's, his eye on Lon. "I've heated Toby some broth, Charlie. See if you can get him to drink some; maybe a biscuit…"

Charlie's eyes narrowed as he read the man's face; relieved when he saw no anger, just a quiet determination; but a clear indication that Belton had no intention of putting up with any bullshit. He took his leave and climbed inside the wagon, purposefully closing the end flap.

Trace Belden stood for a time, silent, staring at his younger brother's profile, mentally willing the boy to face him. "You were headed home, Lon," he said quietly. "That's where we'll all be heading, soon as Toby's up to making the trip. What's the point of leaving if we can make the ride together?"

The boy's brow furrowed as he struggled to find the appropriate words to justify his decision. There were none, at least not any Trace would believe. Stubbornly, he shook his head, whirling to mount the mare.

Trace reached the boy in one long step, grabbing him by his belt and collar: lifting him bodily away from the horse. Hanging on to the kid's collar, he spun him around. "You on the run, Lon?" he asked. He tapped the Colt with his finger. "You get yourself into some kind of trouble with the law, mixed up with some yahoo going to show you the easy way to make a dollar?" The youth tried to pull away. "I asked you a question, Lonny. I want an answer!"

"No!" The boy's response came too quickly. He still could not look the man in the face without having to immediately look away. "No," he repeated, dropping his head.

Belden lifted a hand, cupping the boy's lower jaw with a closed fist, his thumb pressing into the button of his chin. He forced the kid's head up. "You aren't going anywhere, Lon," he said firmly, the words coming softly. "At least, not yet." He stepped back from the youth. "You will be coming home, back to the ranch; and Toby will be coming with us."

"I sent for McLane!" Lon backed away, the mare preventing his full retreat. "I went to Fort Myer, sent a telegraph. I told him the kid was with us." The words poured out of him. About how he'd gotten drunk, sent the wire.

How he'd picked up their trail wanting to be there when McLane arrived; when the lawman finally took the kid, and Toby was out of his life forever.

Belden listened to the boy, listened to the hate and resentment that poured from him. "You're fifteen, Lon. Just what did you plan on doing if weren't coming home?"

Lon was silent a moment. "I got a job," he lied. He was studying the earth at his feet, and he nudged a sow bug with his toe, turning the creature over on its back.

"Doing what?" Belden persisted. "Swamping out a saloon somewhere; playing cook's helper for some trail outfit?" He knew only too well the kind of work that was available for a green kid. "Maybe holding the horses outside some bank, while your *compadres* make some easy money?" His voice lowered. He pointed at the revolver. "Maybe shove that thing in some drunk's back and help yourself to a poke?"

The boy's head snapped up. He was remembering his final night at the Fort, when he'd lost the last of his money in a rigged card game; remembering what he'd done to get that money back. It was as if Trace had been there, looking over his shoulder. "Maybe," he said harshly, mocking the man.

Belden exhaled. "You know, Lon, in all the years, I never laid a hand on you. Not once. Not until that night, when you cut the bull loose." He shook his head. "That was a mistake, waiting so long.

"Toby found Solomon at the bottom of a sink hole, Lon, in about three feet of water. He stayed with him, alone, all night, keeping the calf's head up out of the water. And you know what he said when we got him out of the water? '*Tell Lon I found him*'. That's all. He lay in that hole and nearly died, because you cut that calf loose and made him think it was his fault." He raked the boy with a long, ominous stare, the dark circles from lack of sleep giving his face an added severity. "You aren't going anywhere, Lon. You're taking that thing off," he pointed at the gun belt, "and you're staying right here. You need a keeper, boy."

The youth shook his head, his face mirroring the same stubborn determination as his brother. "I'm not stayin'!

And I ain't takin' off this pistol." He grabbed at the gun, his hand knotting around the butt. "You wear one, Trace," he yelled, pointing an accusing finger at the man.

Belden sighed. "I wear one because, after the War, I decided to make a name for myself." He pulled himself erect, staring off into the horizon, not wanting to remember. "Well, I did. And now I spend a lot of time watching my back, wondering when someone…" he didn't finish. "You aren't going to live like that, Lon. God willing, none of us are going to live like that; not anymore." He reached down, unbuckling his belt. He pulled the holster away from his hips, feeling naked. Carefully, he folded the belt around the holster. He hesitated, and then resolutely stowed the weapon in the wagon. He looked up, seeing Charlie's face, shaking his head when the man started to speak. Turning, he again faced his brother. "Take it off, Lonny," he ordered.

The boy stood his ground, his feet spread, this chin lifted insolently. He shook his head, his hand still resting on the revolver. "No," he breathed, the refusal adamant.

Belden studied the boy a long time, his stance, the arrogance. "You remind me of the kid," he said softly, reading the sudden confusion that marred the boy's eyes. "The kid, Lon," he repeated, coaxing the memory. "The boy I hung."

Lon's face colored, and he swallowed. He remembered. All of it. Even the sound of the cottonwood bending beneath the dead weight of two bodies.

"That's right," Belden said slowly, nodding his head. "I think of him. I see his face." His voice lowered. "Every night, Lonny; every night before I go to sleep.

"When you were gone, I kept thinking of that kid; what happened to him. Why it happened." He searched the youth's face, looking for some sign that the boy understood what he was trying to tell him, seeing nothing. "You aren't going to end up like that, Lonny. A body hanging from the wrong end of a rope, the crows picking at your eyes." He moved, suddenly, grabbing the boy's arm with his right hand. With his left, he pulled the kid's revolver from the holster. "I catch you with this pistol again, Lon, I'll whip you." His fingers dug into the boy's arm, holding fast as the youth tried to pull free. "Charlie!" He hailed the man, nodding toward the sorrel. "Put his horse up." He still didn't release his hold on the boy, just held him, his gaze locked on the kid's face. "Lon's staying."

******

Belden and Charlie were on foot, leading their horses, Trace reading sign. "A doe, maybe," he said, pointing to the tracks.

Fletcher nodded. "I hope so. I've had just about all the salt pork and jerked beef I can handle." He laughed. "Have you ever seen anybody eat as much as that kid?"

Belden was still concentrating on the tracks. "Which one?" he asked wryly. "Lon's been eating like there's no tomorrow."

Fletcher was feeling philosophical. "Maybe he knows something we don't," he joshed. "I hear God sometimes talks to fools and dreamers." The man stopped walking, his eyes on the shadows at the mouth of the canyon. He swung his rifle to his shoulder and fired.

The doe bolted, leaping in the air, and then faltered. The animal ran a few paces, and fell. Charlie put down his rifle, wetting his thumb. He drew the digit across the sight, grinning across at his companion. "A mite high," he said.

"High, Hell," Belden snorted. They'd made a bet. Five dollars on who made the first kill. The loser also got to skin out the meat. Trace mounted the bay and sheathed his rifle. "I take it you saw her on one of your wood hunting expeditions," he said.

"Dang right," Fletcher replied, grinning, not feeling the least bit remorseful. "Seen her on and off for the past two days." He winked at the man, pulling himself up in the saddle. "My daddy didn't raise no fool, Trace. Said if I was going to gamble, to make certain I was bettin' on a sure thing and playing with a brand-new deck." He held out his hand. "He said to collect right away, too, just to prevent any misunderstanding."

Belden dug out the cash. Sometimes he felt he would never learn. He nudged the bay in the sides, and trotted in the direction of the dead animal.

Wrapping the hind quarters and the side meat in the scraped hide, they trussed the doe behind Fletcher's saddle. The rest, except for the liver, they discarded. Mounted, they started back to camp; Belden rolling himself a smoke and passing his makings to Charlie. He relished the feel of the smoke against his tongue, wrapping the reins around the horn as he used two hands to light up. They moved at a walk, enjoying the adult companionship and light conversation; unashamed of the fact it felt good to be away from the confines of the supply wagon, the bickering of the two boys.

Toby was on the mend. Lon, reluctantly, was doing what he was told, when he was told. And Belden had learned a great deal about what it meant to be a full-time parent. He stared out through the smoke from his cigarette, his gaze on the foothills to the south. In another day, they would be on their way home.

The pleasant daydream was suddenly interrupted. Belden stood up in his saddle, watching a growing cloud of dust. It was coming closer, a giant dust-devil pushed by the wind. Only there was no wind. The bay began to dance, and Fletcher's big grey came alive. "Mustangs!" Belden proclaimed. He held the bay back, feeling the animal fighting the bit, and watched as the small herd – a rare sight on the Texas plains now – turned and came parallel to where they were sitting.

"Well, would you look at that," Charlie exclaimed, pointing to the stallion at the head of the harem. He straightened, the horses coming nearer, slowing down as they turned again to follow the stream bed that led out of the canyon.

The old stallion, tail and mane flying, slid to a stop. He snorted his suspicions to his mares, holding them back from water. Nervously, the stud paced up and down on the bank, stiff-legged, as if measuring the width of the stream and the distance that separated him from the two mounted men. It was a buckskin. Big, roman-nosed, with black mane and tail and dark stockings. He looked like the mismatched offspring of a feral stallion and a domesticated draft mare, short bodied and broad of chest. A broken lariat hung from its powerful neck, the rope swinging like a pendulum as he strutted back and forth trumpeting his warnings. Belden felt a deep rumbling beneath his legs, the proud-cut bay returning the challenge.

"Good God Almighty!" Charlie was still staring at the beast. "That's the ugliest piece of horse flesh on God's green earth!" His eyes probed the small group of mares and foals. "Jug heads! He's breeding a whole tribe of jug heads!!"

Belden's fingers were on his rope, unfastening the thong that held the lariat in place. Charlie couldn't rope for shit on the run, he grinned. Never could. "First man to get a rope on him sits on his rump while the other one cooks dinner," he said slyly. Charlie didn't know he couldn't rope; at least, he'd never admit it.

Fletcher undid his own *reata*. "You plan on keepin' that old stud for a pet, or we doin' this just to see who cooks supper?"

"Just for supper," Trace answered. "And five dollars," he said, feeling magnanimous.

Fletcher nodded and kicked the long-legged grey into a full run. Together, the two men splashed across the shallow stream, yelling. They charged the herd, scattering the mares and foals as they pursued the stallion.

The horse snaked through the herd, trying to elude its pursuers. They were closing on him, the lithe cowponies cutting in and out among the other animals, enjoying the chase. Belden shook out his loop. He was ahead of Charlie, could hear the man behind him on his left. He tossed the loop, the line singing in the air above his head. And then, with a joyful, good-natured whoop, Fletcher barreled up on his big grey, suddenly coming in on Belden's blind side. He charged in front of the man, slapping the bay's nose with his coiled rope. Belden's gelding sun fished as Charlie raced forward to close in on the mustang's right. Neatly, his loop settled over the buckskin's head. They ran along together, topping a slight grade.

The buckskin stallion paced himself, his stride easing as soon as the rope settled around his neck. Charlie dallied the rope and yanked the grey to a sliding halt, gravel flying as the horse set back on its haunches, the man waiting for the sharp jerk that would come when the slack snapped tight.

The jolt never came.

The stallion wheeled around, head down and neck extended, its ears flat against its neck. He was running, picking up speed. Fletcher's grey was still backing up, trying to pull up the slack. It kept backing, Charlie fighting to untangle the rope from the saddle horn. The buckskin bore down on the man and his horse, purposely charging the grey. Belden kicked at his bay and shook out his rope a second time, watching in amazement as the big mustang continued its charge. "Charlie!!" The stallion plowed into Fletcher's gelding at a full run, his massive chest striking the rearing horse in the side and hind quarters.

There was a great cloud of yellow dust and gravel as the two animals collided, Belden's vision blurred by the bits of flying dirt. Instinctively, he covered his good eye, knowing for a brief instant the horror of being totally blind. The dust was settling as he lifted his head, the terrified scream of an injured animal ringing in his ears. The buckskin thundered away, the mares and foals following in the stallion's wake.

Belden look up to the place where the two horses had met. It was empty. There was nothing there, just the barren horizon above the embankment. He kicked the bay in the flanks, digging his spurs in and racing up the incline. Dismounting on the run, he raced to the edge of the chasm, dropping down on both knees as he viewed the carnage.

Charlie was below him, underneath the gelding. The grey was struggling to stand up, but was unable to rise. Belden swung back aboard the bay, a sick feeling at the pit of his belly as he guided the horse down the side of the incline, moving at an angle until they reached the bottom.

The grey was still on its side, its legs flailing wildly, close to Fletcher's head. "Trace…" the man's voice called out to him; distant, weak. Belden pulled his rifle from the sheath beneath his right leg. Aware of the sound as the cartridge slid into the chamber, he levered the rifle and aimed. He shot the grey, dropping the rifle as he dismounted and sprinted to Charlie's side. Frantically, he began digging at the gravel under the man's hips. Then, grabbing Fletcher's shoulders, he stood up, pulling the man free.

Fletcher was chalk white, his bad leg smashed at the hip, a piece of ragged bone protruding from the flesh beneath his torn pant leg. He coughed, blood coming at the corner of his mouth, bright red blood. There was a hollow sound as he breathed, and he blew sand and gravel from his tongue. He motioned Belden closer. "You lost the bet, Trace," he laughed. "When you cook my venison, I want it done. Well done." And then he died.

Belden wrapped the man in his poncho, burying him next to the water, well above the stream bed. He was overwhelmed with a feeling of loneliness; and sat for a long time beside the rock cairn, his right hand resting on the stones that covered Fletcher's face. They had been friends for more than twenty-five years; had grown up together, gone to War together. He tried to think of a time in his life, of a day, that Charlie hadn't been there.

He couldn't remember any.

CHAPTER 15

———

Lon snuck away from camp early in the morning, Charlie's old army issue Henry tucked under his right arm. He wasn't trying to run. After one fool-hardy attempt, he knew better. But he still had to get away; away from all the *yes, sirs* and *no, sirs*, and from the morose, black mood that had plagued Trace since Charlie's death. The man was silent, uncommunicative; unrelentingly stern. He moved and breathed, and went through the motions of being alive, but he was like a dead man.

Toby had been awake as Lon was preparing to leave, his eyes big when he saw that he intended on taking the rifle. Lon thought about the kid. They bunked together in the wagon, and at first he had thought the boy was nothing more than a royal pain in the butt, just like before. He never shut up; always telling Lon how glad he was he had come back, and how happy he was that he was staying. And the questions!! The kid was full of them; hundreds of them.

Lon grinned, remembering the second night he had been back. He'd told Toby about all the things that had happened while he was gone (except, of course, about sending the wire to McLane); about the drinking and the cards. About the little red-headed whore who had taught him how to kiss with his mouth open.

About robbing the drunk. He'd spilled the beans about that one before even realizing what he had done. So he made Toby swear in blood that wouldn't tell Trace; and the kid kept his word. It wasn't so bad, he decided, having him around. It was, he reasoned, like having a kid brother. No better and no worse.

The young man was on foot, his destination no place in particular as he continued his explorations. Still, he was surprised when he found himself beside the stream, next to the pile of stones that marked Charlie Fletcher's final resting place. The rifle he was carrying suddenly felt heavy in his hand, and he canted it against his right shoulder. He didn't know what to feel, thinking of the old man dead. Charlie had always been there; like Trace, always telling him what to do, what not to do. He wiped a hand across his nose. Somehow, he had always felt that Trace and Charlie would never die.

"Lonny," the voice said softly.

The youth turned, his fingers tightening on the stock of the Henry. "Marshal," he greeted, staring up into Mc-Lane's face.

The lawman looked behind the boy, at the rock monument at his back. "Trouble, Lonny?"

The boy followed the lawman's gaze and quickly suppressed a smile. "Toby," he lied. He looked up at the lawman, his face cherubic, fighting the smile while secretly congratulating himself on such a clever deception.

"Toby," McLane repeated. He mentally worked the thing over in his mind. The smile that was tugging at the kid's lips was understandable. He'd been green-eyed as a fishwife from the get-go; jealous of Trace's relationship with the boy. But the grave. "That's a lot of rock for a runt," he observed. The lawman dug into his vest pocket, extracting an old cob pipe. He scraped out the interior of the bowl with his long thumbnail. "What happened?"

"The fever," Lon answered quickly. "All the rain." He shrugged. "Trace was sick, too," he added, his face mournful.

"Um-hum," the marshal grunted. He tamped the tobacco into the pipe and stuck the stem between his teeth. "I guess I made a long ride for nothing."

"Yeah," Lon said smugly. He stared up at the man. McLane was looking at the horizon, his eyes fastened on a spot somewhere above and behind the kid's head. Or so it seemed.

McLane sucked on his pipe, his hand cupped around the match. "Heard you picked yourself up a handgun at the sutler's store out at the old fort, Lon." He watched the boy's face. "Even after Trace took the one away from you at Cutter's." He noted the flush on the kid's face, the embarrassment. "He take that one away, too?" The goading was intentional, and it hit its mark.

Lon's spine went rigid. "No," he said, doing a poor job of keeping the anger out of his voice. He bit his bottom lip, picking the next words carefully, not sure of the man's game. He hefted the rifle. "I'm hunting food, marshal. Don't need a handgun to hunt food."

The lawman nodded. "You said the kid had the fever?" he asked, quickly changing the subject. There was a brief look of confusion on the boy's face, marring the smooth forehead. McLane continued. "Be a shame to come this close, and not drop by to tell Trace hello, give him my condolences." He pointed at the grave with his pipe. "Reckon he'll miss the boy," he finished.

Lon took an anxious step toward the lawman's horse,

his face white. "Mr. McLane," he began, contrite. "Trace doesn't know I sent that telegraph," he lied. "He was going to bring Toby back, once we got the herd to Laredo." He nodded at the grave, his mind racing, the words coming fast. "We had a fight, me and Trace. About the kid. That's why I sent that telegraph…" he didn't finish, his voice filled with remorse. He swung his head back to the law-man. "I'd appreciate it if you didn't tell him…"

I just bet you would, the lawman thought. He decided to play the kid's game. "You'd rather I didn't see him," he said, watching the relief that flooded the boy's face.

"That's right, Mr. McLane," Lon replied, his tone properly respectful. "I was wrong about Toby," he said. "I told Trace that." He cast a sad eye toward the grave. "I just wish I had the chance…" His voice drifted off. "Trace has had more than his share of grief." That part wasn't a lie. "A lot of it was my fault…" That wasn't a lie, either, although the boy wasn't ready to admit it.

The lawman scratched at the day-old beard his chin. "Guess there's no good to come from adding to a man's misery," he said solicitously, "you bein' so sorry about all the trouble you caused." He turned his horse around, lifting his hand in a gesture of goodbye.

Lon watched as the lawman departed. He could no lon-ger control his need to laugh, the sound pushing up from deep inside his chest. He'd been worried about McLane, about what would happen when he showed up; and now he didn't need to worry anymore. He had buffaloed the old fool; had led him down the primrose path. He could hardly wait to brag to Toby about what he had done.

******

McLane had pointed the chestnut to the northeast, towards Liberty. He continued to ride in that direction until he was sure the kid wasn't watching him, and then he doubled back. The boy had been lying through his teeth. Why go to all the trouble of sending the telegraph, and then tell all the lies? Lon had done the thing out of pure meanness; and now there was this complete turnabout, and the story the boy was dead.

The lawman shook his head. There was no small boy buried in that grave. But who? And why? No matter how he added things up, they didn't tally. He was aware of trouble between Trace and Lon, just as he was aware of the kid's having run off. Lon had cut a wide path when he ran, and had gotten himself into more than one scrape. He had screamed to the world that he was going to make his brother pay. And now this. McLane cursed. Trace. Toby. Lon. But most of all at himself, for his insatiable gut need to know the answers to all the questions that were plaguing him.

******

Lon ducked down among the rocks, hearing the sound of shod hooves, his first thought of Trace, the man angry, coming after him. He flattened himself against the rocks and then peered out between a cleft in the sandstone boulders. It was McLane! The lawman's horse was moving at a slow walk, the man relaxed, almost – it seemed – sleeping. He cursed, waiting until the lawman passed his hiding place. *You bastard*, he sore. *You lying bastard!!* The man was going to talk to Trace, to tell him God only knows what. Carefully, he drew bead on the man's broad back.

McLane was on immediate alert, the metal click of a rifle being cocked exploding against the quiet, awakening the stark memories of a man too many times the hunted.

He flattened against the gelding's neck, urging the horse into a run, the animal bolting forward.

Lon fired, the single shot reverberating against the rocks that surrounded him like a clap of thunder, the sound rolling at him from all sides. He saw the horse lurch, falter, and then crash to the ground, the lawman pitched forward and onto the graveled pathway. The youth braced himself against the boulder at his back, his heart pounding, a cold sweat drenching his back and forehead. He stood there, breathing hard, forcing his racing heart to slow. Cautiously, he peered above the rocks, levering another shell into the chamber.

The lawman was sprawled on the ground, quiet, his arms extended above his head. Lon waited for what seemed an eternity, watching the man. There was no movement, no sign the man was alive. Panicked, the boy moved, away from the stand of rocks, the rifle heavy in his hands. He began to run, fast at first, then slowing to a steady dog trot, the fear leaving him. He felt a strange elation, a lightness of body and soul. He had stopped McLane; had stopped the lawman from dogging them, from finding the boy..

******

Belden look up from the fire, watching as Lon strolled into the clearing. He nodded at the rifle. "Toby said you went hunting." There was no anger in him. "Any luck?"

Lon shook his head. He levered the rifle, emptying it, and shoved it back inside the wagon. He held up the collection of ammunition. "Took a shot at an old buck," he lied. "Missed him."

Trace nodded. "We're going home, Lon." He poured himself a cup of chicory. "Toby is well enough to travel now," he said, his gaze on the southern hills. "Come morning," he said softly, "we're going home."

Lon nodded his head, relieved. He wanted a lot of miles between himself and this place, a lot of miles.

******

"It's Marshal McLane," Toby shook Lon hard, whispering.

Lon raised up on one arm, still not fully awake, his mind fogged by the whiskey he had pilfered after Trace had gone to sleep. He grabbed the boy's shoulder. "What?"

"The marshal…" the kid answered.

Lon pulled the boy down into the wagon bed, and then rose up on one knee. He looked out into the clearing, his visibility limited to the narrow opening between the canvas flap and the raised tailgate. Using two fingers, he opened the flap just a bit more. He could see Trace's back, and as he shifted, the campfire, and finally, the figure of the lawman. He strained to hear, shushing the boy, and then dropped back down into the wagon bed. Hurriedly, he began rummaging through the litter on the wagon floor. His cavy sack, the kid's blankets; Trace's slicker. Groping beneath the heavy coat, he found what he was looking for.

"No!!" Toby's fingers closed around Lon's arm, his lips trembling as he watched the youth rise to his knees and strap the gun belt in place. "Trace said if you took that again, he'd whip you!!" He was remembering his own thrashing. "He will, Lonny. I know he will!"

Lon ignored the kid's warnings. "You stay here, Toby," he said. "Pretend you're still asleep." He scooted around the boy, climbing over the seat at the front of the wagon and noiselessly dropping to the ground.

Stealthily, the boy worked his way down the far side of the wagon, staying in the shadows. He came up beside the water barrel, listening intently to what was being said, and his hand resting on the butt of the pistol.

McLane's back was to the wagon. He was unwrapping the cigar Belden had given him, his weight on his right leg. "…and then your little *proscrito* shot my horse." He bit off the end of the cigar and spit it on the ground. "I don't like walking, Trace. I've never liked walking."

Belden stood in front of the man, feeling naked, his hand drifting to his empty hip. It was an old instinct, that dark part of his past that refused to leave him. "He said he took a shot at a deer…"

"And you believed him?"

"I didn't have any reason not to, Linc," Belden answered. He lifted his hand to his head, raking his fingers through his hair.

"That kid's headed for trouble, Trace." The lawman shook his head. "Big trouble…"

Lon stepped out from behind the wagon, his pistol drawn. "It appears to me you're the one headed for trouble, old man." He was shaking, trying hard not to. "Get out of the way, Trace," he order softly.

Belden half turned, facing the boy; careful to stand so that neither Lon nor the lawman were on his blind side. "For Christ's sake, Lon. Don't be a fool…"

"He's the fool," Lon retorted, nodding at the lawman. "I told you the kid was dead!" He waved the revolver at the marshal's belly.

"Yeah, Lon, you told me." McLane yawned. "Only I didn't believe you. You're a poor liar, boy. Among other things." The lawman's voice was filled with contempt.

Lon tilted his head, his eyes cold. "You know, old man, I thought it would be hard to kill you. I really did. But then I drew bead on you…" he shrugged, a smile pulling at the corner of his mouth. "It was nothin', old man. Nothin'."

Belden felt sick. He turned to face the boy fully. "Put the gun away, Lon," he said quietly. The youth shook his head.

"You listen to him, son," McLane suggested. "You listen to him real good." He glanced at Belden. "I want to see Toby," he said.

"Shut up, McLane," Lon warned. "You aren't going to take the kid," he said quietly.

The lawman snorted, angry. "And if I'm so inclined, boy, just who's going to stop me?" He thumbed his nose at the youth. "You!?"

"Linc," Alarmed, Belden turned back to the marshal.

"He doesn't scare me, Trace," McLane said matter-of-factly. He struck a match beneath his thumbnail, puffing on the cigar. "Now, if it was five, ten years ago and that was you standin' there with that pistol," he eyed the man through a thin screen of smoke. "You don't know about the old days, do you, Lon?" he asked, shifting his gaze to the younger Belden. "Trace was a pretty fair hand with a gun back then," he mused, remembering. "More than fair," he finished.

Belden's gut was tied in a tight knot. McLane was playing with the kid. "You're in over your head, Lon," he took a step towards the youngster. "Listen to me," for the first time he saw that the young man had failed to cock the weapon. "You're playing a game you don't know anything about, with a man who helped make the rules. You haven't got a prayer, Lon," he cautioned.

McLane dropped his cigar, his right hand close to his belt. "What he's trying to tell you, boy, is that it's a hell of a lot different taking a man down when he's lookin' at you." He swept the boy with a long, menacing stare, his voice whisper quiet. "Now, your brother there," he said, indicating

Trace with a slight nod, "he could do it." The lawman's right eyebrow lifted when he saw the look of surprise on Lon's face. "Put the gun down, Lonny," he said, tired.

"No," the answered, waving the pistol at the lawman's gut.

McLane inhaled, shaking his head. "I don't want to kill you, Lon," he breathed. "But if you don't put that gun down, I will."

"Lon," Trace pleaded.

"No!!" The kid backed up a pace, his eyes on both men. "He'll take Toby," he said miserably.

Belden took another step toward his brother, placing himself between the boy and the lawman. "You can't stop him, Lon." Trace's voice was firm. "*I* can't stop him!!" He took still another step, his hand extended.

"I can kill him!" The boy's panic was growing.

"No!!" The word exploded from Belden in a hoarse whisper. "Listen to me, Lon…" He stared into this brother's face, advancing again. "He means what he's saying."

Lon's face crumpled and he fought hard to control his shaking fingers. "He's going to arrest me! Put me in jail!!"

"He'll kill you, Lon," Belden declared flatly. He cast a brief glance at McLane. "I know him, Lon. I've known him for a long time. He'll do it."

Lon swung his arm toward the lawman, and found himself face to face with a black hole, the barrel of the .44 aimed at his belt buckle. He had not even seen the man draw. He swallowed, his thumb moving to the hammer of his uncocked pistol.

"Don't do it, boy," the lawman warned. "Don't even think about it." He kept the pistol leveled at the kid's waist. "I really don't want to shoot you." He heaved a great sigh, his chest rising. "I shoot you, then sure as night follows day, I'll have to shoot Trace." He shook his head when he saw the boy's eyes drop to Belden's empty hip. "That's right, son. I'll gut shoot him where he stands, unarmed or no. Because if I don't, he'll come after me, and he'll most likely kill me. You see, I know him, too." He grinned, the smile failing to reach his eyes. "I'm good, Lon; but Trace is better. He was always better."

Lon's eyes were alternating between his brother and the lawman, and he began blinking rapidly. "Trace…?"

Belden's stomach was growling, a burning deep in his gut. He shifted his gaze to the wagon, his eyes narrowing. "He will shoot you, Lon, and then – even if he doesn't kill me – he'll still take Toby. I'll lose you both," he reasoned. He shook his head. "I'd rather lose one of you, than lose you both." He took one more step towards his brother, trying to get close.

Lon's mouth opened, his chin quivering. He stared down at the pistol in his hand, his arm trembling, a shudder coursing through his entire body. Lifting his hand, he drew back, throwing the revolver, watching as it rotated and arced high against the blue sky. It thudded against the ground a considerable distance from the wagon, the dust rising and then slowly settling back into place. The kid faced both men, looking more child than man. "I'm sorry…" He turned, fleeing the place of his humiliation, his arms pumping as he ran from the clearing.

McLane exhaled, easing the hammer back into place. He hefted the .44 in his palm, and then slid the weapon back into its holster. Beads of perspiration appeared on his forehead, and he wiped them away with the back of his hand. "That was close, Trace," he said, genuinely thankful the situation had finally been resolved. "Too close."

Belden turned, his hand stuffed into his pockets. "Thanks, Linc." He nodded toward the wagon. "You'll want the boy now," he said. "And Lon…"

McLane was staring off into the distance. "I don't arrest children if I can help it, Trace. I send them home to their families, with a strong lecture about the value of regular trips to the woodshed. That's something you need to remember." He changed the subject. "The grave?"

Belden inhaled, the pain still fresh. "Charlie. An accident."

McLane nodded. "And Toby?"

This one was harder. "In the wagon." He hesitated, "Christ, Linc. He followed us from Liberty. His mother..." He started to tell McLane about the pony.

"Thinks he's dead," the lawman interrupted. "We had a bad flood, the night of the storm. That's when Toby ran away." He dug into his pocket, taking out his can of snuff. Using the lid, he dipped out a portion, offering it to Belden. Trace shook his head. McLane continued. "We found his hat; that holster and belt the boys gave him, there beside the river. Figured his body had been carried off downstream." He placed the tobacco in his mouth and snapped the tin shut. "They took up a collection at the whorehouse; bought the kid a stone..." He laughed. "Gave that hat of his one of the finest funerals I've ever seen, his Ma all decked out in black like she really gave a damn; the whores wailing and carrying on behind the hearse!" His voice drifted off and he laughed again.

Suddenly, the laughter stopped, his eyes softening as he spied Toby's pale face peering at him from above the tailgate. He waved at the boy. "I'm not taking him back to her, Trace."

Belden couldn't believe what he was hearing. First, the reprieve for Lon, and now Toby. "But you said..."

"I said I wanted to see the kid," McLane butted in. "Lon didn't give me a chance to say anything more." He looked into Belden's face, seeing the questions. "I figured he was dead, just like the rest of them. Didn't seem possible he

could cross that river…" He paused. "And then that telegraph came from Lon, telling how the boy was with you."
He shook his head. "It got to eating at me, how that sprout
could make it out of town, find you and the herd. I had to
see for myself," he shrugged. "Figured that if he made it,
it must've meant he wanted to be with you, and wanted
it bad." He was quiet again. "You know, Trace, I let you
take the kid back to the ranch with you, you're going to
have to keep him hid. Or at least keep anyone from Liberty
knowing that you have him."

Belden nodded. He looked toward the wagon, returning
Toby's feeble smile with a wave of his hand. He thought
briefly of Elizabeth, and their son. *Her son*, he corrected
himself. *Hers and Cord Bishop's*. "I don't have any reason
to go back to Liberty, Linc. Not anymore."

"You're sure?"

"I'm sure, Linc." Belden answered. He rolled his
shoulders, his gaze on the northern skyline. "Tell Cord
it's over," he said. A great wave of something intangible
swept him, and all the old emptiness was gone.

McLane exhaled. "It was over for Cord when he and his
men found the two yahoos you left hanging on that cottonwood, and the two graves." He shook his head, recalling
the look on Bishop's face when he read the note Belden
had left pinned to one of the dead men. *An eye for an eye.*
And Bishop had understood its meaning. "It was *you* I was
concerned with, Trace. You've hated Cord for a long time."

"It wasn't worth what it almost cost me," Belden said
quietly. "What it did cost." He was thinking not only of Lon
and Toby, but of Poke Williams and Delgado. And in a way,
he supposed, Charlie. *The wrong place at the wrong time.*

McLane reached out, clapping his broad hand on Belden's
shoulder. "Well, I got me a town to run, Trace," he said.

"And I sure in hell can't do it from here." He extended his hand, taking Belden's. "You owe me a horse," he grinned.

"Lon owes you a horse," Trace said, correcting the man. He pointed to the sorrel mare.

The lawman laughed. "I'm taking his tack," he announced. He had no intention of prying his own saddle from beneath a dead horse.

******

Belden went to the place where Solomon was tethered and pulled the rope loose. He led the animal to the back of the wagon, tying him off next to the gelding. McLane had been whistling when he rode off, the high-pitched warble of a man mimicking the calls of wild birds, and Belden could still hear the sound. It was growing fainter.

"Trace?" Toby pulled himself up, his chin resting on the closed tailgate. His eyes searched behind the man, probing for McLane.

"Yeah, son," Belden answered, enjoying the sound of the word.

"Marshal McLane?" the boy asked timidly.

Belden grinned, thinking of the man. "He's gone back to Liberty, Toby." He pulled himself up into the wagon. "You feel like taking a ride?"

The boy hesitated, and then nodded, his shoulders sagging. "Yes, sir," he said softly. Belden was going to take him back; had to take him back.

Belden touched the boy's cheek and then moved forward to the wagon seat. He paused, his hand on his bedroll. He could feel the stiff leather of his holster beneath the woolen blanket, his fingers tracing the outline of the gun butt. It was no good to him, wrapped away like some boy's hidden treasure. He was a long way from being a boy, and even farther from a boy's games. It would be different for Lon and Toby; he would see to that. But it was too late for him. He unlaced the blanket. The pistol had been a part of him too long. Resigned, he strapped the belt and holster back into place on his hip, the weight good against his right thigh.

Unwinding the lines from the brake, he climbed over the seat and settled himself onto the hard boards. Gently, he slapped the leather across the backs of the two draft animals and urged them forward. The team moved out, their wide hooves slapping against the dry ground.

Lon turned, facing the sound of the approaching team. Squaring his shoulders, his pushed himself away from the small *palo verde* tree, waiting.

Belden pulled the wagon to a halt. He sat for a time, staring down at his younger brother without saying anything. His eye drifted to the ground. Lon's pistol lay in the dirt between them, the steel barrel glistening in the sun.

Lon followed his brother's gaze, his brow knotting as he debated his next move. He lifted his head, his mouth dropping open as he saw Belden's gun belt. They exchanged a long, silent glance, Lon unable to meet his brother's slow scrutiny. He stared at the ground again, working the thing over in his mind. At last he understood. It was more than seventeen years that separated them. Trace had grown up in a different time, in a different way. *I'm good, kid*, McLane had said. *But Trace is better. He was always better.* Lon knew that somewhere, sometime, there was going to be someone that would want to know just how much better.

Slowly, the kid unfastened the buckle of his gun belt, feeling the empty holster slide away from his right hip. He doubled the belt over, hesitated, and then – stepping over the pistol – thrust out his hand. "You said if you ever caught me wearing this again," he lifted the offending strap, "you'd whip me." He swallowed, his eyes on the man's set face. "I guess this is as good a time as any…"

Belden raised his right hand and pulled his hat far down on his forehead. He stretched out the arm, flexing it to its full length. "I guess it is," he said quietly, nodding his head. He slid across the seat and jumped down to the ground. Reaching out, he took the belt; standing tall above the youth, the leather strap slapping ominously against his right thigh. There was a grim satisfaction in him as he watched his younger brother die a thousand small deaths in anticipation of what was coming. *You deserve this*, he thought. *For all the hell I know about, and all the hell I can only guess at.*

There was noise, a rustling behind the canvass, and Lon tore his eyes away from Trace and the damning belt. Toby's head poked out from behind the driver's seat.

"Toby!" Lon stared at the boy for a moment, and then shifted his gaze back to his brother. "McLane," he said weakly. "I thought…"

"McLane's gone. Back to Liberty," Belden said. "On your sorrel, with your tack." He turned then, staring longingly at the rolling foothills to the south. "It's a long walk, Lon." He reached up, scratching at the spot on his cheek bone where the eye patch rested. "If I were you," he advised, "I'd climb aboard this wagon and hitch a ride home."

There was a long respite as the boy absorbed his words. "Home?" the youth asked, still not believing.

Belden grinned across at his brother, and then up at Toby, the smile creasing the skin behind his ears. "That's right, Lon," he said softly.

"Home."

A Look At: The Dundee Saga

THE DUNDEE'S ARE FIGHTERS, AND THE BLOOD-BATH HAS BEGUN!

Bound by blood but separated by years of hatred and mistrust, half-brothers Jonathan and Cooper Dundee are locked in a fierce struggle over their father's legacy—the Dundee Ranch and the failing transport company.

With cruel cunning, Jonathan has launched a ruthless plot to betray his family and to gain control of everything. All too quickly, the long-simmering rivalry becomes a deadly wave of kidnapping, and murder that threatens the Dundee family, and soon escalates to include the entire Arizona territory.

Old wounds are opened as the brothers square off in a high-stakes power struggle for the Dundee dynasty.

"Brace yourself for a tough ride you won't soon forget."
The Dundee Saga includes: Tucson and Casa Grande.

AVAILABLE NOW ON AMAZON

About the Author

Kit Prate has always been a fan of Western fiction, but also tends towards anything on the written page that strikes her fancy.

Kit grew up as a curious child in a world of curiosity; blessed with parents who shared their sense of wonder in the small things, and a dry, mid-western sense of humor.

Luckily, marriage and work provided an opportunity to travel all across the US and into Mexico. That made it "easy" to write about places she'd seen and people she was fortunate to meet along the way.

Like a lot of authors, Kit Prate wants to try it all; although preferring the past to contemporary times. Happy endings? Maybe. Skewed logic and complex and conflicted characters, you bet. The world is an interesting place in fascinating shades of grey; not simply black and white.